Winds of
Promise

Library of Congress Cataloging-in-Publication Data
Evans, Shirlee, 1931-
   Winds of promise / Shirlee Evans.
     p. cm.
   ISBN 0-8361-3506-7
   I. Title.
PS3555.V26W56 1990
813'.54—dc20   89-11181
                                               CIP

WINDS OF PROMISE
Copyright © 1990 by Herald Press, Scottdale, Pa. 15683
   Published simultaneously in Canada by Herald Press,
   Waterloo, Ont. N2L 6H7. All rights reserved.
Library of Congress Catalog Card Number: 89-11181
International Standard Book Number: 0-8361-3506-7
Printed in the United States of America
Cover art by Edwin Wallace
Design by Jim Butti

96 95 94 93 92 91 90 10 9 8 7 6 5 4 3 2 1

To Julius Luoma
1900-1988

Wyoming trapper, rancher,
friend

Contents

1

Festering Resentments

The damp gray of day deepened to dusk as a shroud of mist silently embraced Solomon Timins' farmhouse, fading yet another November day to night. Splotches of housing developments, their streetlights winking on to outline twisting lanes of pavement, snuggled in on three sides of what was left of Sol's farm. An island of acres was all that remained now on either side of the old, squared-off, two-story white house.

Sol sat in the lighted kitchen of the home his father had built years before. Idly he watched his son, now well into his middle years, putter around the outdated electric cookstove. Vic reached into the hot oven to retrieve a single store-bought frozen dinner, jerking his hand back to grab a soiled pot holder from a wall hook.

"Well, at least it's hot," Vic muttered, sliding the steaming plate off onto the range top. Gingerly he peeled back the cover, glancing at his father. "Are you ready to eat?"

Sol, who had recently reached his seventy-sixth year, was attired in his usual faded blue bib overalls over a tan shirt frayed at both cuffs. He sat at the round kitchen table leaning on his elbows. An edge of gray horse-shoed his balding head. He had not moved, choosing to ignore the question.

"Dad? Did you hear what I said?" Vic was all but shouting now.

"I heard," Sol grumbled.

"Well?"

"Well, what?"

"Are you ready to eat?"

"Wouldn't be sittin' here if I wasn't."

Vic's form appeared lean and well put together in his blue jogging togs. Sol never knew what to expect from Vic in dress or deed these days. But then—he never had understood his son. Even as a boy.

Glancing at Sol, Vic placed the steaming plate on a pad in front of his father. "Do you want anything else? I could fix a salad. I bought lettuce and tomatoes for you the other day."

Sol shook his head.

Vic stood back as Sol stared down at the limp vegetables and pale potatoes, with thin slices of roast beef floating in a transparent gravy. Sol sighed, picking up a fork. "Go on home, Vic," he said as he lifted a forkful to his mouth.

"How about some milk? You drink way too much coffee." Vic turned to rummage through the refrigerator. "Looks like I'd better pick up some more milk. Anything else you need?"

Sol chewed with deliberateness, staring off at a corner of the large kitchen.

Vic turned, raising his voice. "Dad. I'm talking to you."

"Don't need nothin'."

"I could hang around awhile if you'd like."

Sol shook his head. "Go on home. Likely Nina will be settin' my phone to ringin' pretty soon, wonderin' where you are."

"Can you—?"

"I can take care of myself," Sol interrupted. "Was doin' it fine long before you come back here."

At last Vic walked to the door. "Don't forget to turn the television off tonight. It was on, you know, the other morning when I came over to find you still in bed."

Sol put his fork down as the door closed behind Vic. "It's a wonder he don't try spoon-feedin' me." He glanced down at the food in front of him. It really didn't taste all that bad. It was just that he had no appetite tonight. He pushed himself out of his chair, picking up the plate as he reached for his cane with the other hand. Thumping his way out to the back porch, Sol scraped the food off into the dog's dish, scooting the dish with his cane out the door onto the top step.

Back in the kitchen he filled the empty plate with water, leaving it to soak in the sink. He headed then for his favorite chair in the high-ceilinged, narrow-windowed living room. He usually watched television before going to bed. Tonight he was especially tired. He wasn't sure why. He hadn't done much. Sinking into the chair Sol watched the television screen without really seeing it, allowing his mind to drift back. Seemed that was where his mind was most of the time these days.

He thought of his father, Victor Timins, who had died forty-eight years before, his farm passing on to Sol, his only child. Sol farmed the land for nearly forty years after his father's death. Then, just nine years ago, he sold off all but twelve acres. It seemed much longer than that now.

Two hours later Sol awoke. He got up, turned off the television, and went to bed. Tomorrow was another day. "I wish it wasn't. Wish I didn't have to see it," he muttered.

The next morning Sol was up earlier than usual. He would fix his own breakfast and eat in peace before Vic showed up. He felt more rested this morning. As soon as he finished eating he pulled himself to his feet, retrieving his cane from where he had leaned it against the table. Sol shuffled his slippered feet across the worn linoleum, carrying his bowl and spoon to the sink. He went back to the table and drank the last swallow from his cup.

He was about to set it down when he stopped. "I'll probably want more when I come back in from the barn," he said aloud. "Then—maybe I won't." He hesitated, looking back at the sink. "Maybe I should wash the dishes before I go feed the cattle."

Sol's shoulders sagged at the prospect of such a momentous decision. "My Friend," Sol complained again to his God, "seems I can't decide even these trifles any longer. Can't understand why you don't bundle me up and take me on home like you did Ruth."

He closed his eyes as he stood there in the kitchen of the old house where he had uttered his first piercing wail as an infant. He was the last of his family, except for his son and daughter and his grandchildren. Little good they were to him, though. He had never been close to his children or to theirs.

Although, he had to admit, Vic did seem to be trying lately. Trying too hard to suit Sol. Janet, his daughter, lived in the East now. She called on his birthday and at Christmas. It had been a long time since he had seen her or her family.

As for Vic, Sol wished he were not so close. He was thankful Vic had returned from the Middle East before any harm could come to him due to the upheavals over there. He just wished he had not offered Vic that land to build on.

Sol recalled how he and Ruth had missed their only son when he first went overseas as an executive for an American-owned oil company. Ruth had especially missed him. Now, after she was gone, Vic had come back to the western slope of the Oregon Cascade Mountains with a new wife. A second wife. Nina, who was young enough to be Sol's granddaughter. Vic had taken an early retirement supported by stock in the oil company. It was just that he lived too close.

"There's no more warmth in that boy than there was in my own father. Should never have named him after his grandfather. Seems handin' down the elder Victor's name only gave my Vic cause to follow his grandfather's stiff-necked ways. Another mistake, my Friend. Seems my life lately has been one mistake after another."

Deciding at last to leave his coffee cup on the table, Sol went out to the back porch where his jacket hung on a peg above his rubber barn boots. "Can't figure you out, my Friend," Sol rambled on. "Can't figure why you'd let me to make the mistake of lettin' Vic build so close. It's as if my father had come back to hound my steps again after all these years."

He pulled on his heavy red-and-black-plaid jacket, settling a stained green-billed cap over his balding head. Kicking out of his slippers he was about to push his feet into the boots when he noticed the rusted coffee can on the floor filled to the brim with water. He remembered then, he had heard it raining during the night.

"Should have checked that can first thing when I got up. Can't remember like I used to," Sol muttered. "Have to write myself a note, I guess. Leave it by the kitchen sink."

Sol stooped carefully to pick up the can. He opened

the door to pour the rainwater from the leaky roof onto what remained of Ruth's flower bed as a gust of wind splashed water back on him. Glancing up, he noticed the sky was clearing, revealing patches of distant blue. Although the rain had stopped, tiny transparent water globes still formed at the ends of the bare, twisted branches and twigs of the great oaks in the backyard.

Sol's work-round shoulders slumped, shrinking his normal five-foot eight-inch frame. His once-firm confident stride, as he worked his land and fed his family, worshiping his Friend Jesus in his own special secret way, was gone. He realized his physical deterioration had accelerated since Ruth's death the year before.

"It was Ruth who had made life worth livin'," he noted to himself. "Ruth was the one who warmed this old house into a home. She was the one who convinced me to sell the milk cows when we reached Social Security age, pointin' out how we'd been tied down all our married lives after comin' back to the farm when Dad died." Sol smiled. "Seems like centuries ago. Didn't want to come back here, but there was Mother and the farm to see to. The curse of being an only child, I suppose."

He shook his head. "Was a mistake leavin' the raisin' of the youngsters up to my mother and wife those early years while I tended the farm. By the time Mother was gone, I was just a shadow in Vic and Janet's lives."

He smiled as he thought about his and Ruth's conversations when he reached sixty-five. Ruth had talked on and on, about how they could travel now and do things they had never had a chance to do before. It soon sounded good even to Sol, and so he sold his milk cows. But after just two trips by car—one to the East Coast to visit Janet—he decided roaming the country was not for him. And so he went out one day, without telling Ruth, and bought ten head of beef cattle. The day they were trucked in, he informed Ruth if she wanted to continue traveling she would have to do it without him. He recalled her reaction now.

"She surely did surprise me," he said. He was accustomed to conversing aloud with himself and his God. "She seemed downright relieved, goin' back to raisin' a garden again, cannin' more food than either of us were able to eat." Sol had to admit he was glad the milk cows were gone. He did not miss those daily, damp, before-dawn excursions to the barn during Oregon's long winter months. The mixed bunch of beef cattle gave him just enough to do.

A jab of pain nudged his remembering as his mind brought him to the happenings of the past year. As suddenly as his father had been struck down, Ruth was taken by a stroke. In a matter of hours she was gone. He recalled the funeral, burying her without support from either of their children. The people of their church—Ruth's church actually, since he seldom attended—and a few neighbors stood by. They brought in food and tried to make him feel he was not alone. But he *was* alone.

Janet called a couple of times. Her first call came soon after he informed her of her mother's death. She told him it would be difficult to take time off from her job right then and so she would not be able to fly out for the funeral. He had never been able to free himself from her words, even after a year had passed: "I can't do anything for Mom now anyway." Didn't Janet realize *he* might need her?

Sol tried reaching Vic at the time, but somehow the news never filtered down through the company's ranks to his son until after the funeral. They reported he was off in the desert backcountry of some strange sounding Middle Eastern country. Vic finally phoned the evening after his mother's body was laid to rest. At the end of their conversation Vic informed his father he figured there was no sense in coming home now, since everything had been taken care of. He was trying to wrap up the loose ends of his work before taking an early retirement. He assured his father that he would visit within a few weeks.

The hurt stabbed deep whenever Sol thought of it. So much that he mentioned his disappointment in his son and daughter when Pastor Brock stopped by the day after the funeral to see how he was getting along. At that time the minister tried enticing Sol to church. But Sol didn't feel right about going without Ruth. He had never been a regular at the Community Church down the road. Not like Ruth and his mother. He knew Ruth longed for him go with her, but he was usually able to find an excuse. He wasn't sure why, exactly. He knew and worshiped the Lord. He just didn't feel comfortable in church. Now, after Ruth's pasing, it seemed wrong to hustle off to church when he had not seen fit to go with his wife and family.

As Sol's mind flicked back through the events of the past year, the Marshes came to mind. At the time of Ruth's death their closest neighbors, Perry and Vera Marsh, were in the process of moving to town after selling the farm joining Sol's to the back. Sol had few close friends. He had always been a loner, except for God, with whom he had privately conversed down through the years. He had been closer to Perry than to any of the other neighbors. While the Marshes did what they could for him after Ruth's death, he realized they had all they could handle with their own uprooting at the time. Knowing Perry and Vera were not living across the back field any longer had added to Sol's sense of loss.

He realized he had been only going through the motions of living since Ruth's death. The cattle had to be taken care of, the house kept in some kind of order, food cooked, and the dishes washed from time to time. He'd learned to run the clothes washer and dryer after some trial and error. But his spirit was not in any of it. Just getting out of bed in the mornings was more of a chore than milking a barn full of cows had ever been in times past. The corners of Sol's mouth, a mouth that had once turned up in a quick smile, now sloped downward, the creases at the corners of his eyes falling to the same pattern. There was simply nothing to smile about any longer.

As he came back to the present, he found himself still standing in the open doorway with the empty coffee can in his hand. "Better put it back under the leak," he spoke. "If I don't I'll probably forget when it starts rainin' again."

He pulled on his boots and picked up his cane, making his way down the back steps and out through the yard. The grass was now ragged and unkempt on either side of the path.

"Should have mowed it before winter set in, with that new mower Vic bought after mine was stolen," he observed. "Grass is all full of bones and trash carried in by Jake. Should have gotten rid of that old dog. Jake's like me, long past being good for anything."

Sol paused at the garden patch in which Ruth had once labored so lovingly, buttoning his jacket against the bracing fall wind. Year-old stalks of corn lay rotting in the weed-choked rows. Volunteer potatoes had risen from the debris during the past growing season. But Sol had not bothered to harvest them. They were Ruth's. Ruth was gone.

Placing his cane with care on the worn path, his body swaying with a recently acquired shuffling gait, Sol made his way toward the sprawling red barn. He'd always found comfort there. It smelled of hay, cows, and life. It was still in fair shape. Ruth used to razz him about that.

"You farmers are all alike," she would say, a spark flashing in her gray-blue eyes. "You take better care of your barns and animals than you do of your houses and families."

But that was not the case. Sol knew she had not meant it. Their home had always been a landmark of dignity in the community. Until just recently he had maintained the place with pride. But since Ruth. . . . Sol trudged on. He didn't want to think about it anymore.

The two story barn had been gutted of most of Sol's milk-cow equipment after the animals were sold. He had torn out the stanchions, converting the space to a cattle feeder. He traded his large farm tractor for a smaller one with a front-end blade to scrape the feeder clean every few days.

Sol entered the barn, his cane giving off a hollow sound on the floor, echoing against the wide-boarded walls. He made his way to where the beef cattle awaited their morning ration of alfalfa. Their throaty lowing called out their impatience with the man. A pile of hay rustled in the corner as Jake, Sol's off-breed old Collie, pulled himself awake and stretched. The dog came to him, greeting the man with a half hearted wag of his hay-matted tail.

A fat, reddish brown, speckle-faced steer thumped into the manger, shoving a smaller black one away. Sol noted the manure piling up. "Should clean it out. Should have done it a couple days ago, my Friend." He sighed. "Maybe tomorrow. Don't feel much like it today. Can't stop thinkin' about Ruth. Was just a year ago today. . . ."

Jake followed Sol to the ladder leading to the hayloft above. He'd already fed the last of the hay bales he had pushed down two days before. He would have to climb up and pitch some more over the edge. Propping his cane against the wall, he slowly climbed the ladder to the loft. He had been climbing that ladder all his life. Vic worried that he might fall, and yet Sol felt more at ease on the ladder these days than he did on solid ground.

At the top he began rolling the bales of hay to the edge, letting them fall with a soft thud to the floor below. Jake edged out of the way, used to the routine after all these years. Sol counted the remaining bales. "Better order more," he noted aloud. "Shouldn't have let that housing developer talk me into selling off my land. Could have raised all the hay I needed. Another mistake, my Friend."

As soon as the cattle were fed, Sol headed back toward the house with Jake ambling behind. He knew he shouldn't be feeding the overfat canine twice a day. Ruth had insisted Jake be fed only once. But Sol didn't think it mattered much now if Jake was too fat. "You've earned a bit of enjoyment," he said to the old dog. "Got no one else to spend my money on. Might as well let you enjoy the best."

Sol paused by the pump house. He looked out over what was once his farm, the wind plucking at his clothes. Beyond his remaining field all he could see were streets, cars, and houses—houses holding transplanted city folk with kids who climbed his fences and orchard trees, stretched the barbed wire between his fence posts, and broke the limbs on his fruit trees. Only a few acres remained of the once-thriving eighty-acre farm, since he had sold most of the land to a fast-talking developer. There were also the three acres he had signed over to Vic after his son's return. Sol turned, glancing toward Vic's sprawling new brick house to the north. He had not set foot inside Vic's house since he and Nina moved in. He sighed, shaking his head.

"Never should have given him that land. Forgot how ornery the boy could be. Guess he's not a boy any longer. Forty-nine his last birthday, if I recollect right. Too old to be marryin' a girl of thirty-five. Don't know why Vic had to go and divorce his first wife, leavin' her with three young ones." Sol tried to calculate the ages of his grandchildren. "Guess they aren't so young anymore, either."

He resumed his walk back to the house, passing by the open garage where his car was stored. He stopped driving when Vic came back and took it on himself to do everything for his father. Sol reached the house with Jake and was about to climb the steps to the back door when he heard a car coming up the long driveway.

He waited, leaning heavily on his cane. "With any luck, Jake, it won't be. . . ." But it was.

2

A New Neighbor

Vic's red sports car swept around the corner with a scattering of gravel as it slid to a stop by the back porch steps. Sol watched with expressionless eyes as his son untangled himself to emerge from the small automobile.

"Morning," Vic greeted as he walked toward his father.

Sol had to admit, his son certainly did not look his soon-to-be fifty years. An English-style billed cap all but covered Vic's wavy sand-colored hair, now flecked with gray. A red knit shirt, under a tan corduroy sports jacket, topped tight-fitting brown slacks.

"How are you this morning, Dad?"

Sol ignored the question, asking instead, "How come you're out so early?"

"It rained pretty hard last night." Vic's voice rose a pitch. "I thought I'd better come check that can under the porch roof leak. The floor will rot out if it keeps running over."

"I emptied it."

"Did you eat breakfast?"

Sol pretended not to hear. It saved a lot of needless conversation, letting Vic think his hearing was about gone. It was no business of Vic's if his porch floor did rot. "I was just about to feed old Jake," Sol muttered as he turned to climb the steps, easing himself up with the aid of his cane.

Vic followed Sol and the dog in the house. "Why don't you feed Jake outside. He smells like a barn."

His father gave no indication he'd heard.

"What did you eat this morning?" Vic walked to the kitchen sink, glancing at the dishes there. "Cereal and coffee aren't enough. How about some scrambled eggs? I'll fix them."

"Got no eggs," Sol declared.

Vic opened the refrigerator. "There's still that dozen I bought the other day. You haven't used a one."

Shuffling to the refrigerator, Sol stooped to reach for the carton. "Maybe Jake would like a couple raw eggs with his hamburger. Be good for him."

Vic turned away, shaking his head. "You take better care of that dog then you do yourself."

Taking a pound of hamburger from the refrigerator shelf, Sol crumbled the meat in a dish, adding the two eggs.

"We had a call last night from Nina's father," Vic commented. "He's coming to stay with us for a while. I've told you about Frank. We were in the Middle East together. Worked for the same company."

Sol nodded.

"We've been friends for years. That's how I met Nina."

Ignoring Vic, Sol continued with Jake's breakfast, taking the dog's dish out to the porch. Shuffling back to the kitchen, he poured himself a cup of coffee and sat down at the table without offering his son either coffee or a chair.

"Did you hear what I said, Dad?" Vic asked, raising his voice a notch.

Sol nodded. "You said Frank was comin'. Nina's father."

"I told him I had some work to do on your place. He offered to help. I wanted you to know I'll soon have that leak fixed. Think I'll look into some other repairs, too, while Frank's around to help."

Taking a sip of the now-lukewarm coffee, Sol remarked, "Be fine if you fixed the leak. Don't need botherin' with anything else."

"I've been thinking about modernizing the bathroom."

"Like it fine the way it is," Sol noted. "If you mend the roof I'll thank you."

Vic turned to leave. "We'll see. You will remember to eat lunch now, won't you?"

Sol again pretended he had not heard. "Got to go back out and clean the barn," he said getting to his feet, following his son to the back door. Vic stopped, sizing up the empty coffee can on the floor, checking to make sure it was lined up directly under the widening ceiling stain.

"It's okay," Sol insisted, pushing on past to hold the door open, bucking the brisk wind as it kicked at the fallen leaves in the backyard. "I've got to get out to the barn now." Sol stood there, angry and hurt, waiting for Vic to leave. His son had not said a word about Ruth—his own mother. Maybe their son was too busy to think about her anymore, to remember this was the first anniversary of Ruth's death. Of course, Vic hadn't been around at the time.

The spring on the outer screen door had been unhooked and the door secured back against the outside wall for winter. Sol, his back to it now, accidentally nudged the screen door loose as Vic squeezed past his father. Vic caught it on his way out. He was about to latch it back to the wall when Sol pulled it closed. "I'll take care of it," he said, his tone crisp with impatience.

Vic turned to size-up the situation. "I think I'd better look into putting up a storm door for you, too."

"Screen door's just fine like it is," Sol insisted. "Don't care for those aluminum things they're makin' these days."

Ignoring his father, Vic remarked, "A storm door would keep the draft out when it blows the way it does today. They're on sale in town."

Sol felt his anger boiling to the surface. Vic never had paid attention to him, his own father, even as a child. Sol realized he shouldn't have left the raising of his children completely in Ruth's hands. Before his mother died, she and Ruth had taken responsibility for them, teaching them the rights and wrongs of things. Too late now, he realized he should have had more of a part in their lives.

Sol's own father, the elder Victor for whom Vic was named, had been an authoritative man—unforgiving, unyielding, unbendable. Sol had determined he would never be like that, especially with his own children. And so Sol had stayed out of the rearing of Vic and Janet. He regretted it now. Ruth had earned their son and daughter's respect. He had not. He was, he supposed, paying the penalty for the relinquishment of that God-given duty.

Vic was lowering himself into his car just as Sol was cooling off. "Now you eat lunch," Vic called. "I won't be over the rest of today or tomorrow. Nina and I are going to the coast for an overnight stay before Frank comes. You make sure you eat something. You've got to take better care of yourself."

The anger capped within Sol reached the bursting point. He could feel the heat of it. Ever since Vic moved back Sol had successfully swallowed the resentment his middle-aged son managed to foster within him. He watched now with outward calm as Vic backed the sleek red car around to roar out of sight down the gravel driveway. But inside Sol was seething with a fired-red heat.

His hand still on the screen, Sol stood there trying to bring his anger under control. "I wish my family tree was out there with those old oaks. I'd grab hold and shake till it fairly trembled! I'd prune Vic's limb back till only a twig was left. I'd. . . ." He shook his head. "But then, guess maybe this old branch of mine's most too dried and brittle to do much shakin' an prunin'. I'd just like to be around when Vic's branch grows old and starts to wither. Wonder how he'll handle that?"

Sol's shoulders slowly straightened as he stepped back inside the porch enclosure, yanking at the screen. The frame bounced against the casing. With a snap the rusty bottom hinge gave way, sagging the wood-framed door crazily off center.

A feeling of exhilaration surged through him. It felt good to vent his anger. The last time anger had consumed him was the day he'd left Ruth behind at the cemetery. Hurting and alone that evening Sol had gone to the barn to feed the cattle. In his misery, he threw a pitchfork at a young steer that happened to be in his way. The wound on the animal's shoulder required a week of washing and medication where the sharp tongs had penetrated. Sol was so distressed over taking his hurt out on the animal that he resolved never again to lose his temper.

He smiled to himself now. This time it had felt good! However, he figured he'd probably given Vic even more reason to replace the screen door with one of those glass and aluminum contraptions.

"I've done it again, haven't I, my Friend?" Sol

mused. And yet the smile remained. The creases at the corners of his mouth and eyes turned up, lighting his face with life once again. It had been a long time. "Haven't always managed to do right. Even though I've tried ever since takin' you as my special Friend while still a lad. Seems there's somethin' in the Good Book that turns a green light on righteous anger. And right now I'm feelin' mighty righteous!"

Still smiling, Sol stepped back into the house. He had no intention of cleaning the barn that day. "Just wanted to get rid of Vic," he said to Jake as the dog licked his bowl clean, scraping it across the floor with each swipe of his tongue.

Across the field Vic entered the back door of his own house. Nina looked up and smiled as she emptied the dishwasher. She brushed her dark hair back from her forehead, and stepped toward him. "What's the matter? Had another run-in with your father?"

Vic sighed. "Why can't he understand I only want to help? Everything I say, everything I do, he takes as an affront to his pride." Vic's shoulders slumped. "I'm going to give up one of these days. I'll sell the house and we'll get out of here the way Janet did."

"You left, too. Remember? But you came back."

"I know. . . ." He hung his jacket on the back of a chair, turning to take her in his arms, burying his face in the sweet smell of her hair. "I don't know how much more of this I can take."

"It can't be easy for him, either," she reminded.

Vic dropped his arms from around her and turned to the window, staring out at the racy lines of his car parked in front of the garage. "He realizes his memory isn't what it once was. I suppose it *is* hard on him." Vic turned to Nina again, raising his hands in a helpless gesture. "But I can't help him. He fights ev-

interest brightening his eyes.

Stopping, Ted turned back. "There's getting to be quite a few draft horses again, especially in the Midwest. Some small farmers are using them in place of tractors. But to most people they're just a hobby. I've had saddle horses since I was a kid. I've never owned draft horses, but I've always wanted to."

Sol's interest had been struck. He leaned against the doorjamb, his mind going back to the days when his father had farmed with the big horses. Sol had, too, for a time, until tractors became the thing.

"Ever driven a team?" Sol inquired.

"A few times." Ted shoved his hands into his vest pockets. "I helped a neighbor with his, back in Iowa."

"Didn't know there were many around, let alone bein' used." Sol rubbed his chin in thought. "Especially around these parts. You say they're a hobby now?"

Coming back to the steps, Ted placed a booted foot on the bottom platform. "They sure are. They've got draft horse clubs and put on shows, plowing matches, that sort of thing. Some people have thousands of dollars invested in their animals and equipment. I can't go into it that big, but they do have farm classes where the wagons and harnesses aren't so fancy."

"Ever handled the lines of a runaway team?" A hint of a smile pulled at the corners of Sol's mouth. "I recall a team of bays my father owned. Ran away with him and the manure spreader early one spring mornin'. Tore the spreader to pieces and nearly killed his best mare. It was the first and only time I ever saw my father shaken. Always used to think he could master anything and anyone till then. I was young when it happened, but I recall feelin' a bit of comfort findin' my father mortal, like the rest of us." A chuckle rose from Sol's throat as the picture of the incident flicked through his mind.

"I've seen a couple runaways," said Ted, "in the show ring. Makes you realize how much power you're trying to control with a thin set of leather lines."

Sol had been sizing up his new neighbor. "What was it you had in mind, rentin' my barn, I mean? I've still got cattle."

"I know," Ted replied. "I'd just need a couple horse stalls and a small lot to turn them out in. I thought, if you didn't mind, I might fence off a corner of your pasture on this side of the barn."

Sol stepped out of the house, allowing the screen to sag behind him. "There's four horse stalls left." "Been using 'em for storage. Always meant to tear the partitions out, but never got around to it. Used 'em for calf pens when I was still milkin' cows. Suppose I could let you rent a couple. The outside door's been nailed shut, but that could be opened up. Don't guess the cattle would miss a bit of pasture."

Ted tilted his hat back with a forefinger. "But do you think having them here on your place would cause more trouble with the neighbor kids?"

Sol eyed the younger man. "Could cause you trouble if the hoodlums start snoopin' round. They'll steal you blind if you leave things out. I've learned that the hard way. Had a lawn mower taken right out of my front yard last summer."

"I know. I've lost tools from my open garage during the day. Kids get bored and start looking for trouble—if it *was* kids."

"Never should have sold my land. Wouldn't have if I'd known what it was gonna be like," Sol commented.

"My own two youngsters are seventeen and twelve. The girl's the oldest. She has other interests now, but she used to be quite a horsewoman. The boy still likes them. He misses the saddle horses we had to sell when we moved out here. I was hoping to get him involved so he'd have something to do to keep him out of trouble."

Sol's eyes narrowed. "Wouldn't want your boy hangin' round all the time. Don't know but what he's one who's been raisin' cain around here."

"If he has, he'd better not let me catch him!" Ted responded. "I won't stand for that sort of thing. He knows better. My wife and I both work, but Kathy—that's Teddy's sister—keeps an eye on him until we get home."

Sol ran a hand back over his balding head. "How much were you expectin' to pay for the use of my barn and pasture? You'll need a part of the loft for hay, too."

"I'll pay whatever is fair," Ted offered.

"Wouldn't want your boy bringin' any of his friends over. Be best, I'm thinkin', if he didn't come 'less you was with him."

"I was hoping Teddy might be able to feed the team right after school. Before I got home. The responsibility would be good for him. But. . . ." Ted turned thoughtful. "He could wait until I got home I guess. I understand how you feel."

At last they agreed on a rental fee for the stalls and pasture. As Ted turned to leave, Sol called after him, raising his voice above the wind's rush. "You picked out your team yet?"

Ted stopped, his hand on the truck door. "I'm going to look at a couple this weekend." He hesitated. "How would you like to come along? I could use advice from someone who's owned drafts."

Unable to remember how long it had been since

anyone had shown an interest in his opinion about anything, Sol replied, "I wouldn't mind goin' along—if you think I'd be of help."

"Good." Ted was smiling. He appeared pleased. "I'm not acquainted with the draft horse people in Oregon yet, so I've got no one to go to for advice." He opened the truck door and climbed in. Stretching his head out the open window, he called, "I'll be back tomorrow evening to start work on the stalls."

Sol watched as Ted backed his truck around and drove off, scattering the oak leaves in the yard. With a glance skyward he smiled as a gust of wind brushed him. With it came a strong sense of promise for the future. Was it a sign from the Lord? he wondered. Ted coming just when he did? "Well now, my good Friend. Things just may be pickin' up around here!"

3

Chicken Man's Revival

All afternoon Sol's thoughts kept going back to the big horses he had owned and worked, bringing the past so close he could almost smell the sweat and feel the lines tug between his fingers. It helped keep his mind from drumming up visions of Ruth.

The next morning he hurried out to the barn. He would begin getting ready for the horses himself. He wouldn't wait for Ted. Moving faster than usual along the path, Sol found himself putting less weight on his cane. He smiled when he noticed a car parked by the barn. The man standing beside it was looking off across the field.

"Well," Sol greeted. "What you doin' way out here, Perry?"

The heavyset red mackinaw-jacketed man turned. "Morning, Sol. Just looking out over where my place used to be." He shook his head, running a hand back through his thick shaggy mass of gray hair. "Can't bear to drive by there anymore, what with the buildings all gone."

Sol stopped beside his former neighbor. He sighed. "Did you ever think we'd live to see this?"

Perry shrugged. "We did it, you know. We sold them the land. It was you and me."

Sol nodded. "I still think it was a time of muddle-headed weakness. And we weren't the only ones. There were the Mayfields and the Smiths. We all sold about the same time."

"The money looked too good," Perry acknowledged, "after digging out a living all those years. It saved having to pay taxes on land we didn't use. You sure didn't need all the land you had for those beef cattle you bought after selling your milk cows."

"I know. But it just doesn't set well. Not well at all. Doesn't feel right puttin' an end to a whole way of life." His regrettable action in selling off the major portion of his land, bringing the ever encroaching housing developments in closer and closer, was a definite point of annoyance to the aging widower.

Changing the subject, Sol commented, "Haven't heard from you for a while. What's the occasion?"

"I. . . ." Perry hesitated, looking Sol squarely in the eye. "Vera and I got to thinking at breakfast this morning. It was just a year ago yesterday that Ruth passed on. Must have been a bad day for you."

Glancing away, Sol felt moisture brim his eyes. "It hasn't been easy." He looked at Perry then. "Was good of you to remember. Good havin' you stop by."

Seeming ill at ease, Perry placed a wide hand on Sol's shoulder. "How about coming back to town with me for dinner? The wife's cooking up a roast with browned spuds and carrots just the way you always liked."

"I'd better not. Don't drive anymore since Vic's back. Haven't had the car out of the garage in months."

"I'll bring you home later."

Sol was shaking his head. "Thanks anyway. Tell Vera I'm grateful. Some other time maybe."

They talked awhile, then Perry left. It had helped,

having someone besides himself remember Ruth's passing. He just wished Vic had recalled the date.

After feeding the cattle, Sol poked around through the clutter that had been pushed off into the horse stalls over the years. As he sorted through the odds and ends, he started a pile of throwaways. Be nice, he thought, having the big horses around again. He'd enjoyed working them in the old days. His mother used to tell about her grandparents coming to Oregon in the 1800s, walking beside a covered wagon pulled by three yoke of oxen. She revered the old ways. He supposed he had inherited a bit of nostalgia from her. The old ways were a part of their heritage, after all.

Jake lay in his favorite corner watching Sol work, waiting for the breakfast his master had apparently forgotten. By noon Sol had one stall cleared out. Slowly he stretched the kinks from his back. "Been a long time, my Friend, since I worked this much." A smile brightened his eyes. "In fact, this is the first time in weeks, months maybe, I've been hungry. Think I'll fry up some of that hamburger I bought for Jake. Need somethin' to stick to the ribs, workin' like this. Hamburger sandwich would go right good about now."

He glanced toward the cattle feeder as he left the barn. "Should have cleaned the runway. Have to get at that tomorrow. Come on, Jake. You must be as hungry as me."

Sol was more keenly aware of what remained of his farm as he and Jake walked to the house. The fruit trees in the orchard needed pruning. The neighbor kids had been sneaking over, climbing the limbs and breaking them down. Actually, he didn't care about their taking the fruit. He didn't use it much anyway. What he didn't like was people coming onto his property without asking, showing no respect for what belonged to him.

Sol stopped. It appeared as though someone had written on the old chicken coop with black spray paint. "Now what they been up to?" he wondered aloud as he walked toward the small weather-bleached building, pushing aside the crumpled, rusty-wire mesh fence with his cane. There on the building was scrawled: "Old Grumps is a Chicken Man!!!"

Shaking his head, Sol turned, ambling to the house. "Chicken Man, am I? I'd like to fricassee their drumsticks." The thought brought a reluctant smile. He wondered if he should add that to the vandal's artistry.

Once in the house Sol took a good look at himself in the fade-blotched bathroom mirror as he washed. He didn't much like the man he had become during the past year. His face was thinner, edged with lines. His balding head, fringed with all that remained of once-thick brown hair, was nearly white. He had been noticing the change in his reflection over the past few months. But now a new image was staring back at him. Life? Could that be what it was? Was that actually a spark glistening there in his eyes?

"Haven't much liked growin' old," Sol remarked to the image before him. "Up until Ruth died, I never really thought of myself as old."

After eating twice as much lunch as he was accustomed to, Sol headed back out to work on the horse stalls. His gait quickened on the path. Nearly gone was the shuffling of his feet. The slope to his shoulders was not as pronounced either.

Sol pulled the nails out of the door leading to the pasture, then stepped off an area he figured to let Ted fence. When Ted came by that evening, Sol was still busy in the barn. "Decided to let you use all four stalls. Be no extra charge. You can store your harness and things you'll be needin' in the other two."

Ted unloaded a stock-watering tank from his truck, placing it in a corner of the pasture. "I didn't intend for *you* to do all this work," he told the older man.

"Things here you wouldn't know what to do with. A lot of it needed throwin' out. Thought I'd best do it myself."

By the time Ted left that evening Sol was bone-weary. He walked slowly to the house, sinking deep into his favorite chair in front of the television news before cooking supper. He was hungry when he awoke an hour later.

Sighing, he pulled his stiffening body up out of the chair. "Guess I'll scramble some of those eggs Vic's been so worried about. No sense givin' them all to Jake."

After a meal of eggs, toast, and applesauce—some Ruth had canned two years before—Sol remained at the kitchen table until a knock sounded at the front door. Folks seldom came to the front of the house. With an effort he stood up, his body aching from his long day's labor. He picked up his cane, crossing the living room to the door.

It was dark outside. Sol was a bit leery opening the door. A person heard so many stories. He switched on the porch light and looked out through the door's lace curtained square of a window. A middle-aged man in a dark suit smiled in at him.

He relaxed, unlocking and opening the door. "Well, Pastor Brock. Never expected it would be you." He held the door open wider. "Come on in."

The minister was far from handsome. Nothing like those slicked-up preachers Sol sometimes watched on

Sunday morning television. The minister's thin face appeared too narrow for his long, hooked nose. His smile made up for his lack of eye appeal, however.

"I realized this evening," he began, "it'll be a year ago tomorrow we had the service for Ruth. I thought maybe you could use some company tonight."

"I appreciate that," Sol noted with feeling. "Come on out to the kitchen."

After depositing his supper dishes in the sink, Sol poured coffee into two cups, sitting down with a sigh across from his visitor.

"How have you been getting along, Sol?" the pastor inquired. "It's been awhile since I came by to see you." He smiled. "And you haven't seen fit to visit us at church."

"No. Never was what you'd call a churchgoer. Not like my Ruth used to be. But I've never forgotten the good Lord. Don't think he's forgotten old Sol, either."

"I'm sure he hasn't."

"God's not only at church, you know." Sol tapped his chest with a finger. "He's right here with me all the time."

The minister nodded. "But I would think you'd find comfort in attending worship service with us. Just being with others would be good for you. Besides, we'd like to get to know you better."

Sol sighed again. "Maybe. Someday. Right now—well, I'm just not ready. Ruth got used to goin' alone. She asked me time after time to go with her, but I hardly ever did. Don't seem right now, goin' without her."

"I suppose," Pastor Brock responded. "Remember though, we're there if you need us. Just don't neglect the Lord, Sol, or his Word."

As soon as the minister left, Sol went straight to

bed. It seemed that every joint in his body blazed with fire. And yet he could not remember when he had felt so satisfied with a day. "Good to have somethin' to do again, my Friend. Didn't know I still had it in me."

Sol caught sight of his old black leather-bound Bible, now filmed with dust, as he reached to switch off the bedside lamp. He used to read some from it nearly every night before Ruth came to bed. Lately he hadn't felt much like reading anything.

Ruth always read hers aloud at the breakfast table. "The day goes better when you start it with the Lord," she would say.

He figured she had no idea how close he was to his Maker. He never said much to Ruth about his faith—never mentioned how he had picked up the habit as a boy of talking things over with his Friend, thanking him, or asking for help. Sol had been afraid she would think him weak if she knew. He still felt the ridicule his father had heaped on his young shoulders after catching him in the hayloft one day, pouring his soul out to God. And so he had pulled back, content to leave his family's spiritual lives in Ruth's hands. Now, it seemed, he was paying the price.

He reached for his Bible. Flipping it open his eyes glided down over the words of Psalm 92, describing the righteous in God's eyes. The fourteenth verse grabbed his attention. He stopped to read it again.

"They shall still bring forth fruit in old age; they shall be fat and flourishing."

"Can't say I'm fat *or* flourishing, my Friend. According to Vic, I'm wasting away to nothin'. Brings me food. Practically stands over me while I eat." Sol chuckled to himself. "He should have seen what I put away today. Maybe there *is* worth left in this old shell after all. I've felt better today than any time since Ruth passed on."

Sol closed his Bible thoughtfully and turned the bedside light off, easing his stiffening frame under the covers. "Don't think I'll let Vic know about helpin' Ted. Not for a while. He thinks I can't take care of myself. Best to keep my mouth closed and my eyes and ears open around Vic and that new wife of his. Learn a lot more that way, I've found."

The next morning as he made his way to the barn, Sol's body echoed with pain from the previous day's work. "There really does seem to be life left in this old man, Jake," Sol said to the dog as he broke a hay bale open for the cattle.

He was walking back to the house with Jake trailing behind when he noticed Vic's car turn into the driveway. Sol patted the dog's head. "Don't forget, Jake, we're both about ready for the boneyard. No sense in Vic knowin' everything."

The small red car approached at a slower speed than usual. Sol waited, his hand resting on Jake's head. Vic stopped in front of his father. Both car doors swung open at the same instant. Vic emerged from the driver's side as another man, a bit older, lifted his ponderous frame from the other.

"Morning, Dad," Vic called as he walked toward his father. "It rained last night again. I hope you're keeping an eye on that can under the porch roof."

Sol allowed the remark to wash over him. He had checked the can first thing when he got up. "Been rainin', you say?" Sol questioned in a thin voice.

Vic stopped in front of him. "Dad, I want you to meet Frank. Nina's father."

The man had followed to stand behind and off to one side of Vic. Sol figured him to be well over six feet tall. While Vic was still lean and muscular, Frank appeared mushy soft, a roll of fat bulging over his narrow belt. Sol guessed him to be in his middle fifties, five or six years older than Vic. It was the man's eyes that grabbed Sol's attention. They were small, set back in the flesh of his checks. Sol could not detect their color. They were not eyes you looked into, but resembled slits of glass shuttered behind a glaze of ice.

Frank extended a puffy hand. Sol took it, allowing his own to go soft in the man's firm grip. "You and Vic been friends a long time, I understand." Sol raised his voice as he had heard others do who were hard of hearing. "Vic have a hand in raisin' Nina, did he? Before he changed wives, I mean?"

Vic shifted his stance as Frank stared at Sol. "Nina's mother and I divorced years ago. I seldom saw my daughter until she was grown. If you're thinking she had something to do with the breakup of Vic's first marriage, you're dead wrong!"

Vic gripped Frank's arm. "Dad wasn't implying anything. He's. . . ." Vic lowered his voice. "He's not been thinking too clear lately."

Frank nodded, without diverting his attention from the older man. Sol hunched over his cane, leaning on it with both hands, allowing his eyes to stare between the two men.

"I brought Frank over so we could size up the work that needs to be done around here. I'll have to order materials before we can start." Vic seemed uneasy.

"I'm goin' in the house now to feed Jake," Sol spoke to no one in particular, waving them off with a hand as he turned toward the house. "Come back some other time."

"No, Dad," Vic said, stopping him. "We're going in

with you to look over the work that needs to be done. We're not leaving yet."

Shuffling away, Sol thumped his cane along the path to the house with Vic and Frank right behind him. Once inside Sol ignored the two men, breaking an egg over Jake's breakfast hamburger, making sure Vic saw it before he and Frank went to look at the bathroom.

Sol was standing by the kitchen sink when Frank came back alone. "I see you've got some cows left," Frank remarked, stopping in the doorway. "I understood Vic to say you'd retired from farming."

Turning, Sol noted, "Sold my cows. Got beef cattle now. Feed 'em, then ship 'em out soon as they're ready for market."

Frank watched Sol without expression.

The older man glared back at him. Sol did not like this man, but he wasn't sure why.

"That land you're using for pasture must be worth a fortune."

"Don't need no fortune. Got more than I'll ever be able to use after sellin' off most of my land—which was a mistake."

"Ever think of selling the rest? Moving to town?"

"Nope! Sorry I sold what I did. Too many houses and people crammed in all around. Too many kids."

Frank appeared lost in thought for a moment. "You know," he began, "you'd be further ahead if you built a shopping center on that land. There are no stores in this area. And, as you pointed out, there are lots of people."

Sol shook his head. "Town's only six miles down the road. Besides, I've got cattle. Don't want to build nothin' else or move anywhere!"

"But—"

"No buts!" Sol cut him off. "Don't want to hear no more about it."

"What's going on?" Vic questioned as he came back in the room.

"I got your dad's ire up. I was thinking aloud about that field he's using for pasture. A shopping center—you know, one of those strip malls with small shops clustered around a good-sized grocery store—would do well here."

Vic glanced at his father, who stood with his back to the sink. Sol looked away, the firm set of his jaw going slack. "Come on," Vic spoke to Frank. "We'd better go. Dad most likely didn't understand what you were talking about. His hearing's so bad he only gets about half of what people are saying."

"But he seemed. . . ." Frank was staring at the older man. "Yah, you're probably right."

"We're going now, Dad," Vic said, raising his voice again.

Sol looked up and nodded, waving the back of his hand toward the door. "Fine!"

He figured they were headed to Vic's place, but a few minutes later he looked out to see them walking into his barn. Hurrying out to the porch, Sol pulled on his boots again. "Better get out there in case they notice those horse stalls been cleaned out. Not ready for Vic to find out about that just yet."

"Dad!" Vic called as Sol pushed open the barn door, his tone braced with irritation. Sol looked up. The two were standing above in the loft. "The hay's about gone. You soon won't have anything to feed your cows."

"Cattle," Sol corrected under his breath. Then louder, "Cows you milk. Cattle you eat. I got cattle."

But Vic was going on, and on. "And it's time you

43

sold them. It's too much for a man your age. You could fall and get hurt out here."

Sol pretended not to hear. When he was younger and exhibited a brash mouth, his mother often reminded him: "Silence is the beginning of wisdom, Solomon."

Climbing down from the loft with Frank following, Vic noted, "Frank will be storing some crates up there for few weeks."

"It might be more like a few months," Frank corrected, watching Sol. "Does anyone besides you and Vic come out here?"

Sol shrugged. He noted they were not asking if they *could* store Frank's boxes, but were telling him they were *going* to. It made him mad. This was his property, after all. His home. Who did they think they were, anyway? He wondered if he should tell Vic he'd rented the horse stalls to Ted, but decided against it.

"Why?" he asked, looking at Frank. "You bring some oil back from the Middle East you want to stash away?"

Frank gave Sol a look that could have gushed water from a rock.

"Dad won't mind if you store your things here," Vic said, raising his voice as he turned to his father. "Tomorrow is Saturday. We'll be back early to start on the porch roof. We've got to leave now. Why don't you go back to the house and rest awhile?"

"Got to clean the cattle feeder," Sol replied. "Didn't get it done the other day." He made a mental note to call and order another load of hay for Monday. He had forgotten all about it.

"Wait to clean the feeder," Vic was saying. "I'll try to do it for you in a couple days. You need to be taking better care of yourself. After the work's done on

44

the house, I won't be running over as often as before while Frank's with us. You are cooking for yourself, aren't you, Dad?"

Sol gave a stony-faced nod while smiling deep inside himself. Now, that was good news, not having to put up with Vic running over all the time for a while.

Frank and Vic headed toward Vic's car as Sol watched from the barn doorway. Then, recalling he was to go with Ted the next day, Sol called out, "I won't be home tomorrow. A neighbor's comin' by. Goin' to take me . . . shoppin'. Probably be gone most all day."

Vic waved a hand to let Sol know he had heard. He and Frank then eased themselves into the cramped little car and roared off down the driveway.

"Wants me to sell my cattle, does he? Wants me to get rid of the only thing that's kept me gettin' out of bed mornin' after mornin' since his mother died. Doesn't seem to realize he's gettin' older himself."

Sol glanced skyward. "My Friend, what I wouldn't give to be handed back a couple minutes of Vic's growin' up. I'd learn him some respect. You can just bet I would!"

4

Partners

The following morning Sol awoke to yet another wet November day. Sodden snowflakes flecked the icy rain outside his steam-streaked kitchen window, promising a complete takeover if the temperature dropped lower. He had come to dread Oregon's chilled winter dampness, especially during the past few years. It awakened his aches to where ignoring them did no good. He pulled an old gray sweater on over his shirt. Ruth had knit it so long ago he had forgotten how many years it had been. He glanced at the calendar—Thanksgiving was only a few days away.

Ted was at his door soon after he finished a hurried breakfast. Teddy, Ted's twelve-year-old son, was with his father. Sol eyed the boy suspiciously, wondering if he might be one of the trespassers stretching the barbed wire between his fence posts and climbing his orchard trees.

The boy appeared quiet and well mannered. Teddy, no doubt named for his father, was topped by thick blond hair that refused to lie flat. It covered his ears and forehead, fringing the intense blue of his eyes.

Sol shrugged into a jacket, following the two out to the barn where Ted had left his truck. He waited with the boy under the barn roof overhang while Ted checked the height of the loading ramp in case they brought a team home that day.

Watching the boy, Sol thumped his cane on the spongy ground a couple of times, Then he asked in a tone intentionally harsh, "You been on my place before?"

Teddy flinched, looking up at the man. The boy's eyes met Sol's before glancing quickly away. Sol waited, staring at him. Teddy shoved his hands deeper in the pockets of a much-worn dark maroon jacket that matched his father's vest. Without looking again at the older man, the boy gave a slight nod.

"That mean you been here?" Sol inquired. "With some of your friends?"

"Yes. . . ." His voice trailed off. "I came with them a couple times. Maybe more."

"Was it you who painted them words on my chicken coop?"

"No!" Teddy shook his head, his damp hair flying like match sticks. "Honest. Dad would tan me good if I did something like that. I took a couple apples once. But they were just laying there rotting. Like nobody wanted 'em."

"What else you and those other kids been doin' around here? Why do you keep pokin' around my place, anyway?"

Teddy shrugged. "I don't know. Most of the guys never been on a farm before. They like lookin' at stuff, wonderin' what it was used for. Like that old rusty disk out in the corner of your pasture. They didn't even know what it was."

"Made you feel like a big man, showin' your friends things they didn't know anything about. That right?"

"I guess," Teddy acknowledged. "But I won't ever come with them again. I promise." He glanced at his father, who was now measuring the height of the truck bed. "Dad told me I wasn't to come without him. He doesn't know I've been here with the guys. Are you going to tell him, Mr. Timins? I'll get in an awful lot of trouble if you do."

Sol gazed long and hard at the boy, his forehead pulled down in a frown. "Did you have anything to do with takin' my lawn mower this past summer?"

"No!" The boy's eyes shot wide again. "We didn't move here till a couple months ago. I don't know anything about your lawn mower. Honest."

Ted was walking toward them. "Ready to go?" he called.

"Whenever you are," Sol answered.

The boy was watching Sol. He edged closer, whispering, "Are you going to tell my dad, Mr. Timins?"

"Not just now. We'll keep it between the two of us for a while."

Sighing, Teddy turned away, his body slumping.

"Let's go," Ted said, pushing his wide-brimmed hat back on his head as he opened the truck door to slide in behind the steering wheel.

"Where are these horses you want to look at?" Sol questioned, climbing in the cab after Teddy.

"North of here. We'll probably be gone most of the day. Hope that's okay with you."

"Fine with me," Sol responded, recalling again that Vic and Frank were due to begin work on his house that morning.

He wondered if Teddy would get bored and mouthy as the day progressed. Or worse yet, get to whining. Nothing he hated more than a whiner. Too bad, Sol mused, they couldn't go on a school day. Too bad Ted had to work during the week. Sol smiled to himself as the truck turned out onto the main road. At least he had something to hold over the boy if need be.

It was noon by the time they reached the first address advertising a draft horse team for sale. The house and a low patchwork-built barn were run down, the yard cluttered with toys. Through the rain Sol could make out the rear ends of a couple bay horses tied under a shed roof. The man who owned them had tried, he told Ted, to horse-log. The horses were a mixed breed. Their owner admitted he didn't know much about handling a team, adding he'd found the logging venture more than he cared to continue. The horses looked as though they were a cross between saddle and draft stock. It also appeared they had not been getting much nourishment.

They did not spend much time there, turning down the owner's offer to harness the team so Ted could try them. At least the rain had let up by the time they left. A few minutes later Sol sat with Ted and Teddy eating a hamburger at a small country junction cafe. "If a man's gonna keep animals, seems he ought to see they're fed proper," Sol remarked.

Within two hours the three pulled up in front of a well-kept farm where, according to a sign by the roadside, the owner bought and sold horses. There were horses everywhere—from a miniature buckskin pony to the team of large draft animals whose advertisement Ted had circled in the folded newspaper on the truck's dash.

The horses were black shires with white markings on their heads and legs. They were half brother and sister, said to be gentle and well broken to harness, although the gelding was snorty. The horse dealer harnessed the tall, leggy black mare and gelding, then ground drove them around the cement surfaced barn lot while Sol and Ted watched. Teddy climbed a wood plank fence to sit out the demonstration. Sol stood below the boy, thankful the rain was holding off. It was getting colder.

The thick-bodied animals bowed solid muscular necks, lifting their hooves high as they took small, ginger steps. The horse dealer walked behind, leaning back on the lines to hold them in. Long white hair grew from below the horse's knees to nearly cover their hooves, shimmering with every hoof fall. Sol glanced at Teddy perched atop the wood fence. The boy watched the animals with his mouth agape.

"The paper didn't state whether they were registered or not," Ted was said to the owner.

"They are."

"How much you asking?" Ted questioned, whistling under his breath when told the price. It was considerably more than he had told Sol he was prepared to pay.

Sol stepped closer, lowering his voice. "They're a whole lot better than that first team you looked at. Didn't see the bays in harness, but I have a feelin' these two are better trained. They're better bred, too. You got no idea how the other team's been handled. Could be soured. Spoiled. Their owner admitted he didn't know much about horses."

"I know," Ted said. "But the price on this team is too high for me. A lot more than I've put aside."

Planting his cane with a firm thud on the ground— the cane he had been carrying on the crook of his arm all day—Sol looked Ted in the eye. He hadn't known the cowboy-outfitted man long, and yet he liked his new neighbor. Ted treated him as an equal, a person whose opinion was valued, which was more than Sol could say for his own son.

"I. . . ." Sol stopped, wondering if he was about to make another mistake. Well, he decided, it wouldn't be the first he'd made. Besides, he thought to himself, can't take a thing with me when I cross over to where

Ruth waits. "How about me goin' in with you on this team? I'll make up the difference and you can use my barn and pasture rent-free. We could be partners. How's that strike you?"

Ted stared at Sol, then shook his head. "I couldn't let you do that. I'm not looking for a handout."

"Didn't figure you were." Sol thumped his cane a couple more times. "I'm more alive today than I've been in months. Be good to help out. And, it'll set you up with a good team right off the bat."

Ted appeared thoughtful. When the horses came around again, he took the lines from the dealer, driving the shires back and forth in the barn lot. At last he stopped, glancing at Sol, who nodded with a wink. Handing the lines back to the team's owner, Ted and the man stood there dickering back and forth until a price was agreed on. With a last look at Sol, Ted pulled out his checkbook, noting they would be back for the horses the following weekend with the rest of the money.

Excitement welled up in Sol as he rode home with Ted and his young son. "They responded real good to your gee and haw. Stopped neat as could be at your whoa. Course, we don't know what they'll do once they're hitched to somethin'. They're a snappy pair. Got a mare, too. Could raise a foal. Maybe two. That way you'd have another team comin' up. Had no idea the price of draft horses would ever climb this high. Sold my last team for under two hundred dollars before I got my first tractor. Nope, never believed work-horses would come back again."

It dawned on him he was rambling. It was as though a dam of self-isolation had burst. He glanced at Teddy, who sat between him and Ted. The boy was watching him. Sol smiled. "How does it feel, owning a fine team like that, young man?"

Teddy grinned. "They're partly yours, too, Mr. Timins."

Sol smiled. "But that's gonna be our secret. You can tell your mother and sister, of course. Don't believe in havin' secrets between a man and his wife. Just don't want others knowin'. Especially my son Vic. As far as anyone else is concerned, that team belongs to you and your dad."

Ted glanced at the older man while keeping the truck at an even speed as they headed home along the rain-washed freeway. "This isn't going to cause a problem between you and your family, is it, Sol?"

"My place and my money are still mine," Sol answered. "Vic may think he's my keeper, but he's not. No need him knowin' everything I do. None of his business!"

It was dusk when Ted turned the truck into Sol's driveway. Sol was tired, and there were still the cattle to feed. With his hay supply low, he had put off the morning feeding in order to stretch what was left until another load could be delivered on Monday. Ted offered to help, and Sol gratefully accepted. He might not have the day before. But it was different now. He and Ted were partners. Partners helped one another.

Easing himself down out of the truck cab, Sol hooked his cane over an arm, heading for the barn with Ted and Teddy following. As the three neared the darkened building, Sol stopped. "Looks like fresh truck tracks leadin' back to the loadin' ramp," he said pointing to the ground. "You didn't back all the way up to the ramp this morning, did you?"

Ted shook his head.

"Don't hear the cattle either. Seems they'd be up around the barn bawlin' their heads off since I didn't feed 'em this mornin'." He moved on, his steps quickening.

Ted and Teddy crowded close behind as Sol pushed the barn door open and switched on the light. Silence greeted them as the three walked to the cattle feeder.

"They're not here." Sol went back to the door and pushed it open again, looking out toward the field. It was nearly dark, but he should have been able to see them if they were around. He turned, walking back to Ted and his son. "Well, they're gone," Sol declared under his breath.

He caught sight of a pair of leather driving gloves on top of the manger. He had seen Vic wear those same gloves just the other day. He noticed then that the manure had been scraped clean from the cement floor. "Yep, they're gone. Lock, stock, hoof, and horn of 'em—all gone."

"You mean someone drove in and hauled your cattle off while you were away?" Ted questioned in disbelief. "I thought your son was to be here all day."

"Did someone rustle your cattle?" Teddy inquired.

Sol was shaking his head. "It's more like a son puttin' his nose into somethin' that's none of his concern. Vic's been after me to get rid of 'em. Thinks I'll get hurt out here. Then he found the hay about gone the other day. I ordered more yesterday. It's supposed to be delivered Monday. Never told Vic. He probably thought I'd forgot, so decided to ship the cattle."

"Does Vic own part interest in them?" Ted questioned.

"Nope. But seems he thinks he owns me and all that's mine. Thinks I can't do anything for myself anymore." Sol kicked a loose board at the bottom of the manger. "Guess I had sort of given up. Probably aged ten years in the one since my wife died. Didn't have anything left to live for except takin' care of those cattle and old Jake."

Sol's voice trailed off as Ted put a hand on his shoulder. "Maybe we can get them back. We'll find out who Vic sold them to and see if you can't cancel the deal."

Teddy moved closer. "Dad will help, Mr. Timins."

His eyes blurring, Sol leaned heavily on his cane as he looked at the boy. "Call me Sol, Teddy."

The boy smiled.

"By the way," Ted was saying, "where is that old dog of yours?"

A chill creased Sol's spine. Vic wouldn't. . . . "Maybe he's up at the house waitin' for his supper. At least, I hope so." Ted and his son hurried to the house with Sol to find Jake lying on the top step in front of the door. The old dog slowly pulled himself to his feet, stretching as though the effort caused pain. Sol stopped to pat Jake's head.

Then he noticed it. Leering down at him was a new aluminum storm door. Sol climbed the steps, opening the new door so Jake could go on into the house ahead of them. As soon as the dog, Ted, and the boy were clear, Sol jerked the aluminum door hard, yanking it closed. It creaked, but remained intact. Sighing, Sol went on into the kitchen with Ted and Teddy following.

A note lay on the round kitchen table. It confirmed what Sol had already guessed. Vic had shipped the cattle that afternoon. Vic's note stated he would take Sol and the check to the bank on Monday. The note didn't mention how much Vic had received for the cattle and at that moment Sol really didn't care.

He sank onto a chair, the note in his hand. "My own fault, I guess. Haven't been myself lately. Should have let Vic see I was comin' out of it for the first time since Ruth. . . . But I didn't. It's been sort of a game with me, makin' Vic believe I couldn't hear or think things through. I've been playin' him like a hooked trout. Only I'm the one who got caught, landed high and dry. Yep, it's my own fault."

"Are you going to let Dad help you get your cattle back?" Teddy asked, standing there in the center of the kitchen beside his father.

"Nope!" Sol let the note slip from his hand onto the table, shoving it aside. "Vic's won this round." He looked up at Ted, a spark of life once again lighting his eyes. "I'm still your partner with those draft horses. Right?"

Ted smiled. "You are if you want to be."

"I want to be."

"I was mulling over what you said on the way home about raising a couple foals. If we had the mare bred early in the spring, then bred her back again after the first foal arrived, we'd have another team ready to break to harness in three or four years. I never thought I'd ever be able to get started this fast, or with animals like the ones we bought today. Couldn't do it without you, Sol. And I'm not saying that just to make you feel better."

The idea appealed to Sol. He smiled. "I'll take that check for the cattle and use it for breedin' fees and things we're likely to need." His excitement was returning. "There's no sense Vic findin' out about it. He'd just better not try anything like this again or he could find himself cut out of my will. Maybe I should tell him that. Let him stew over it awhile."

The Bowens left and Sol washed up at the kitchen sink before frying himself a chunk of meat loaf he had made the day before from one of Ruth's faded recipes. When he finished eating, he decided to see what Vic and Frank had done to the rest of the house while he was gone. He figured the porch roof must have been mended since the coffee can had been tossed in the garbage.

The bathroom was a disaster. The washbasin had been pulled from the wall, still connected to the pipes. It hung to one side like a half severed elephant tusk. A second note was taped to the door.

Dad.
Ran into trouble here. Be back tomorrow to finish. Toilet still works.
Vic.

"Well, he's not gonna work around here on Sunday. Even if I don't go to church or always observe a day of rest." He smiled faintly. "Just about every day's been a day of rest for me until lately." He stood looking at the washbasin. "Let Vic have his fun. Let him put in a new one. But not tomorrow! Wish I could be around when that boy gets old. I surely do."

Sol stomped back to the kitchen. Grabbing the phone off the wall hook, he dialed Vic's number. "Won't have you and Frank workin' here on Sunday," he declared when Vic answered. He didn't mention the cattle and neither did Vic. In fact, Sol was surprised Vic didn't question him about using the phone. He had been pretending lately he couldn't hear whenever Vic tried calling.

Thanksgiving came and went during the week. Vic and Nina took Frank and drove to the coast for the day. It hurt Sol not being asked to go along, although he would have turned the invitation down if he had been included. And yet, at least it would have been

horse dealer noted as Ted secured the tailgate. "The fellow I got these horses from said one of his studs got in with them before selling the team. So the mare here could be carrying a foal."

"Was it a shire stud?" Ted asked. "If it was I'd like to see about getting registration papers if the mare does foal."

The man shrugged. "Have no idea. I'll give you his name and address if you want."

5

Slipping the Tether

The team rode well in the back of the truck on the way home. All Sol heard of them was a stomping of their hooves a time or two. Teddy kept turning to watch them through a narrow slit cut in the truck's stock rack.

"So, we may soon have ourselves three for the price of two," Sol commented with a grin, evidencing his pleasure at the deal they had made.

Upon reaching the farm the gelding lifted his hooves high as Ted led him from the truck down the loading ramp. Sol propped his cane against a back tire and went inside to untie the mare. He rubbed his hand along her thick neck, finding it damp.

"Got a little nervous, did you, girl?" Sol comforted as he eased her around to the ramp. He stopped, letting her look out at her new home, her large dark eyes calm as she took it all in, her ears cocked forward.

Below them, Ted let the gelding trot in a circle around him, holding the end of the lead rope. The black tossed his head playfully, his nostrils flaring, as he reached up and out with his hooves, the white hair on his lower legs rippling with every thud of a hoof fall.

The mare and gelding were well marked, Sol noted.

Both bore white blazes on their foreheads, wide between the eyes running to a narrow strip at the nose. The gelding had a slightly wider blaze than the mare. Their manes were growing out from what Sol figured had been a short roach. The eight or so inches of black hair parted in the middle to fall on either side of their massive necks. The gelding's legs were white from the knees down, while the mare had only three white legs with a hind leg solid black, the only marking to ruin a perfect match between the half brother and sister.

Sol rubbed the mare under her jaw, a lump catching in his own throat. "Beautiful animals," he remarked to Teddy who stood below. "Nothin' at all like the teams my father and I used to work."

"Are ours better?" Teddy asked.

Sol nodded. "A lot better."

The boy smiled.

At last Sol led the mare down the ramp, following Ted, who had started the gelding off toward the barn. Inside, Sol tied her in a stall beside her teammate. The men and boy then stood back to admire their purchase.

"I could make name signs with my wood-burning set," Teddy offered. "Would it be all right if I nailed them to the front of the stalls?"

Sol nodded, without taking his eyes from the horses. It was good having workhorses in the barn again. "What are their names? Did anyone think to ask? When you're drivin' you need to speak to one or the other so we should know their names."

"I overheard Teddy asking before we loaded them," his father spoke up. "What did you find out, son?"

"The mare's name is Bell and the gelding's is Mike."

"Fair names," Sol noted. "Wouldn't want 'em soundin' too much alike. Just confuse 'em."

Teddy ran to the barn door, pushing it open a crack, calling back, "There's a car coming."

"Is it red?" Sol questioned with a suppressed dread.

The boy nodded.

"Oh, well. . . ." Sol sighed as he heard the car come to a stop outside. "Remember now, these animals belong to your dad. I'm just rentin' space for 'em. Understand?"

"Isn't that lying?" Teddy inquired behind half-closed accusing eyes.

"Might be. A bit. Not askin' you to lie, though. I'll be takin' the responsibility."

Frank was with Vic as the two came into the barn, stopping beside Sol, who had not moved from in front of the horse stalls. "Those are mighty big horses," Vic remarked. "What are they?"

"Shires," Ted replied.

Frank stepped back in the shadows. A button-front powder-blue sweater stretched tight across his protruding belly. Vic glanced at his father, who shuffled away to lean against the divider sectioning off the horse stalls from the alleyway. The older man's shoulders slumped again, his eyes taking on a vacant stare.

"I thought you were bringing in saddle horses," Vic noted. "These are work animals, aren't they?"

Ted nodded.

Sol turned to his son. "Ted's bought himself some real nice workhorses," he remarked in a childlike whine. He stepped to the animals' heads, his movements stiff and awkward once again. It was an aged Sol who rubbed Bell's soft nose. "Nice horse. Yes, sir. Ted's got himself some nice horses," he crooned, glancing back at Vic. "Seems I recall havin' horses like these. When you were a boy?"

Vic sighed, his tone patronizing. "Yes, Dad, you had a team a good many years ago."

Frank was talking to Ted, asking what he intended doing with workhorses in this day and age. As Sol listened, he caught Teddy watching him. The boy's eyes were accusing, scorching Sol's conscience.

Vic turned back to his father, raising his voice a pitch. "We're bringing Frank's packing crates over tomorrow. We'll be hoisting them to the loft out of the way. You do remember I mentioned Frank would be storing some things up there, don't, you Dad?"

Nodding, Sol straightened to a more erect posture. "That hay I bought is up there. The hay I ordered before *you* sold off my cattle."

"Why didn't you cancel the order?"

"Told Ted he could have it for his horses."

Sol had kept his feelings to himself the morning Vic took him to town to deposit the check from the sale of the cattle. But he was sure his son realized he was unhappy over the deal.

His shoulders were now stooped again as he tried to ignore Teddy's eyes boring through him. Vic accepted his father's explanation without comment. He probably thought Ted would be paying him for the hay, Sol figured.

As Vic started for the door, he looked back at his father. "We'd like you to come over to the house for dinner tomorrow. You haven't been in our home since it was finished and we moved in a couple months ago."

"Can see it fine from my yard," Sol retorted.

"Dad. . . ." Sol detected hurt in Vic's tone. "Nina's fixing a special dinner since we were gone Thanksgiving and couldn't have you over. I don't want you staying over here alone all the time."

"Was alone last year on Thanksgiving as well as this, if you'll recall."

"I called last year," Vic remarked in his own defense. "I explained why we couldn't be with you. In fact, that was when you offered us land to build on. Remember?"

Sol turned away without response. He remembered all right!

After giving up trying to talk his father into joining them for dinner, Vic said he would bring a plate of food over later. Sol accepted the offer without comment or a thank you.

The following afternoon turned warm and dry with a light fall breeze playing among the still damp oak leaves. Sol went about raking them and the trash from his yard, stopping to eat the meal Vic brought over early that afternoon.

He was tired that night as he fed Jake the leftovers from his dinner plate, keeping the pumpkin pie back for an evening snack before going to bed. It had been a lonely day. At times he had nearly given in and walked across the field to Vic's house. Ruth was so strong on his mind. It would soon be Christmas. He tried not to think about their past holidays together, but it was no use. The memories were etched painfully vivid on his mind. And yet Sol felt being with Vic, Nina, and Frank would do nothing to ease his aloneness.

Although the cattle were gone, Sol still went to the barn every morning, turning Mike and Bell out during the weekdays after feeding them a ration of grain. Teddy—with Sol's permission—was racing over as soon as school was dismissed in the afternoons. Ted insisted Sol let the barn cleaning go until evening. "You've got to save something for me to do," he had told him.

Ted hauled over a set of old harness the day after

they brought the horses home. He had purchased it, he said, at a farm sale in Iowa before moving to the Northwest. Sol pointed out places where the leather was weak and worn, offering to work it over after soaking the straps in a special solution of oil. Soon Sol, with Teddy's help, had the harness apart and soaking in buckets.

Ted was shoveling manure into a wheelbarrow one evening a week after Thanksgiving as Sol watched. "How have you been lately?"

Above them Teddy could be heard thumping about in the loft. Sol leaned on the pitchfork he had been using to shake out a bale of hay. "Fine," he replied. "Been feelin' fine. Why?"

Ted smiled behind his moustache. "I didn't know you before, but Teddy says the kids in the neighborhood call you Old Grumps. Actually, you were a little grumpy that morning I came by to see about renting these stalls. You've mellowed out some since then. At least with us."

"My mind's workin' better now. Got kinda stale from lack of use, I guess. Don't use my cane much anymore either. Put it away in the closet the other day."

Teddy was climbing down from the loft. "You walk different too, Sol," the boy said, interjecting himself into the conversation. "You used to walk like a penguin." The boy demonstrated.

Sol chuckled. "Vic hates it when I shuffle my feet like that. I can see it in his eyes. Guess maybe that's why I do it whenever he's around."

The boy was looking at Sol. "What's in those big wooden boxes in the loft? The ones your son and his friend put up there? There's metal bands around 'em and the tops are all nailed down tight."

"Don't know," Sol admitted. "Some of Frank's stuff."

"I found a pile of leather in the corner under some old hay. Looks like parts off a harness or something."

"I'd forgotten about that. Maybe there's still some good pieces we can use on your harness, Ted."

Teddy started back up the ladder. "Come on. I'll show you."

Sol was close behind, with Ted following. The three squeezed past Frank's crates and the hay bales to reach the darkened corner. Although the light was dim, Sol could tell by the feel that there were still good pieces of leather left on the forgotten bits of harness. Ted dragged the tangle past the crates so they could get them down to take a better look at their find. A buckle caught under a corner of one of the crates, shifting it slightly.

"There's an open space between the boards on this one," Teddy exclaimed as he followed behind his father. "It's broke open. And. . . ." He stopped, one eye squinted close to the break. "It looks like a stack of guns inside. Like rifles."

"Come on, Teddy," his father called, pushing the leather off the edge before starting down the ladder. "Don't be so nosy. Those crates aren't ours."

"But, Dad! I think there's guns in there. A whole bunch of 'em," the boy persisted. He turned to Sol, who had stopped behind him, whispering, "Do you suppose that guy Frank could be a gun runner? I saw a television show about people who do that."

Bending to peer in through the opening as Teddy stepped aside, Sol saw light glint off something that did look like rifle barrels all right. "We'd best keep quiet about this," Sol noted.

Teddy nodded, his eyes solemn. "That makes another secret between us, huh?"

After two days of misty rain that puddled to mud, the next morning the sky was clear. It was with relief that Sol squinted up at the milky-blue sky as he walked to the barn after breakfast. It didn't seem possible it could be December already.

As soon as the horses were turned out to pasture, Sol went back to the house. Deep in thought, going over the things he would need to finish the harness repair, he completely forgot about feeding Jake as he sat at the kitchen table penciling out a list. The old dog, who had followed him to the house, finally gave up waiting on the porch for his breakfast and padded on into the kitchen, hunching down by Sol's chair to look up at his human, whining a reminder. Sol smiled, patting Jake's head. With the dog on the porch again content with his breakfast, Sol went back to finalize the list. Finished at last, he walked to the bedroom, changing to a clean pair of overalls. He then rummaged through a kitchen drawer where an assortment of keys were kept. Locating the one he wanted, Sol stood looking down at the silver-colored metal cradled in his hand before dropping it in his overall pocket.

"Haven't driven the Ford since Vic came back," he mused. "Vic's been bringin' more food in than I know what to do with. Haven't really wanted to go anyplace—until now."

After hustling Jake back outside, Sol made his way to the garage. The dust-shrouded green sedan's engine needed several turns of the key and much pumping of the gas pedal before responding. He sat there a minute before backing the car out, waiting for the motor to warm. "Wonder if this is wise, my Friend. Been leavin' everything for Vic to do. Haven't seen anyone who hasn't come to see me. Guess maybe, though, it's time I broke loose."

He drove the car close to the house where a hose was connected to a faucet and washed the dust from the car. Getting back in he took a deep breath, then aimed the vehicle down the driveway. But as he turned out onto the black-topped road, his confidence crumbled. Sitting ramrod straight with a locked grip on the steering wheel, Sol kept his eyes fixed on the road before him.

Town was about six miles to the south. A car came up close behind, hanging there before shooting on around with a roar. The traffic meeting him was coming at dizzying speeds. As soon as he found a wide shoulder, Sol pulled off and sat there, fingers clenched to the wheel.

His descendants had come to Oregon in a covered wagon pulled by oxen over the old Oregon Trail in the mid 1800s. They'd faced dangers and trials he could only imagine. And now here he sat beside a modern smooth-topped roadway, terrified.

"This won't do," he berated himself. "You've been drivin' nearly all your life, Solomon Timins! Ruth used to brag about what a good driver you were. So get on with it. Finish what you started!"

Checking the rearview mirror, he pulled back onto the road. As the feel of the car grew more comfortable, he increased his speed to within five miles of the posted limit. Slowly Sol's grip on the wheel eased as he cruised along, carefully negotiating the curves of the narrow country lanes. He began to take note of the changes taking place. He couldn't say he liked what he saw. Vic usually took the freeway to town when Sol was with him, so it had been a while since he had been along this route.

It was with a surge of triumph that he at last stopped in front of the hardware store on the outskirts of town. He turned the motor off and slipped the key into his pocket. "Now, that wasn't so bad," he spoke aloud, opening the car door and glancing skyward. "Thank you, my Friend."

A young man stood behind the counter when Sol entered, a bell on the door announcing his arrival. "May I help you?"

Sol stopped, glancing around. "Where's Jim? He'll know what I need."

The clerk smiled. "Jim retired last year. Sold the store to my folks. Evidently it's been a while since you've been in. Is there something I can do for you?"

"Need some buckles and snaps for a set of draft horse harness." Looking up and down the aisles at the neat bins and displays, Sol noted, "Things been changed."

"What sort of harness was that?"

"Draft horse harness."

"I'm sorry. . . . But, what's a draft horse?"

Sol eyed the young man. "Just how old are you, anyway?"

"Nineteen. Almost."

"You know what a workhorse is?"

The teenager nodded.

"Well, that's the same as a draft horse. I'm puttin' together a harness for a team of shires." Sol turned to look at the young man again. "That's a draft horse breed." He ambled down an aisle with the young man following. "I'll need some buckles. Could use a good leather riveter, too, if you got one. And some heavy thread for a hand awl, and. . . ."

The bell on the door jingled. Sol turned as Perry Marsh walked in. "Well, Sol!" the heavy-set man greeted. "Thought that was your car out front. What you doing in town? Didn't think you were driving anymore."

"Decided it was time I did. Needed some things. Can't expect Vic to do everything for me. Didn't know if the old Ford would start or not, but it did. Right off."

Perry looked closer at Sol. "You're looking good. Seems you've gained a little weight. Getting around better it appears, too. Not using your cane anymore?"

Sol grinned. "Retired it. How about goin' over to the cafe across the street for a cup of coffee and piece of pie while this young man fills my order?" Sol turned to the clerk. "Or do you still do that? I mean, put orders together for customers?"

"Sure," the clerk replied with a quick smile. "Be glad to, Pops."

Sol shot him a look that would shrivel a gourd. Pops! Was there no respect at all in kids today?

At the cafe Sol and Perry sat at one end of the counter talking of old times. There were the winters to remember they had weathered together as neighbors, especially the freak tornado that nearly ripped Perry's barn from its foundation. Sol then told of his new venture with Ted and the horses.

Perry listened, remarking, "I never cared much for horses. Tractors suited me best. But I recall how you missed your team. Must be good, doing something again. Retirement's no good, Sol, especially for a man who's spent his life working the ground and seeing to his animals. I never should have sold out and moved to town. Don't let the wife know how I feel, but I miss the chores. She likes going to potlucks at the senior center here in town, so I just keep quiet and tag along. Can tolerate it, I guess, until—well, you know.

Until it's over. After all, Vera tolerated being married to a farmer all those years. It wasn't always an easy life."

"No, it wasn't easy. But it was good." Sol wanted to shake Perry awake, and encourage him not to give up the way he had during the past year. But he managed to keep his mouth shut.

Later, armed with a bag of supplies, Sol slowly drove home. It was good getting out on his own again. Life was still going on beyond the boundary of his property. For a while it seemed as if life had died with Ruth. But it hadn't.

"Sure thankful you sent Ted and his horses to me, my Friend. Much longer and I'd have withered clear away to nothin'. Been feelin' sorry for myself, pure and simple."

When he approached the little country church he had attended as a boy with his mother, and then once in a while with Ruth, he was surprised to see a new building going up behind the smaller white frame structure. He hadn't noticed it when he'd passed by earlier, what with his eyes and attention glued to the road along that stretch. Pastor Brock was outside raking the last of the leaves that had fallen from the big maple trees. Sol pulled the car to the side of the road and stopped.

The pastor looked up, walking over to the car. "Morning, Sol. Good to see you out."

Sol nodded, rolling the window down. "Good to be out. Buildin' a new church, are you?"

The thin faced man glanced at the larger building behind him. "Our congregation has outgrown the old one. What with the suburbs expanding like they have."

Sol grimaced. Those city folks were even changing

his church! His church? The thought took him back. Did he actually think of this as *his* church?

"You'd better come to the dedication in a few weeks," the minister invited. "You might feel more comfortable in the new building, with no memories attached to it."

"I don't know," Sol said. "Never was one to put on a holier-than-you-know-what face just because I crossed a church threshold on a Sunday." He put the car in gear. "Well, better head on home and let you get back to work."

It was well into the afternoon by the time Sol turned into his own driveway. The clear December days were growing shorter, shadows slanting long sinewy fingers across the yard. Teddy came running from the barn with Jake lumbering after him as Sol pedaled the car to a stop in the garage.

The boy was breathless as he ran up to the driver's side. "You weren't here when I got home from school." Teddy panted as Sol got out of the car. "So I went up to the loft to push some hay down for the horses. And. . . ." He stopped to take a breath. "Guess what I found!"

"More harness?"

"No. That broken box up there's been opened. And there *are* guns inside. A whole bunch of 'em. Just like we thought. I didn't break it open, Sol. Honest. Who do you suppose did?"

Picking up his bag of supplies, Sol closed the car door and headed toward the house with Teddy. Jake followed, flopping down in his favorite spot on the porch. "Frank may have come over to check on his things while I was gone. Maybe it was him."

"But where do you suppose he got so many guns? There's all different kinds. Some look real old."

Sol shrugged. "Got himself a collection, I expect. Lots of folks collect guns." Placing the paper bag on the kitchen table, Sol turned to the boy.

But Teddy was gazing out the window toward the barn. "It's your son and that guy Frank." He looked back at Sol with wide frightened eyes. "What if Frank didn't open that box? What if he thinks I did? He saw me up there the other day."

6

Trouble Drifts In

"Are they headin' for the house?" Sol asked.

Teddy nodded, turning back with fear in his eyes. "Maybe I'd better go home."

"No. Stay where you are. You're dad will be along soon."

"But what if they know someone broke into that crate? What if they think it was me?"

"Never mind. I'll take care of it."

The back door opened. "Are you in here, Dad?"

Sol stepped to the doorway between the kitchen and porch as Vic and Frank came inside.

"Thought you might be at the barn, but it seemed deserted out there." Vic's expression and tone were serious. "Frank was over earlier and said you were gone. So was your car. You didn't drive, did you? You haven't driven in months."

"About time I did then," Sol replied with an abrupt nod. "Went to town for some things."

"I don't want you driving, Dad. You haven't been yourself lately. I can take you or pick up whatever you need. If you had an accident and hurt someone you'd never be able to forgive yourself."

"No more likely to do that than you," Sol noted, his eyes narrowing.

Frank stepped closer. "You haven't seen anyone fooling around the barn, have you?"

Teddy came to stand behind Sol, slightly off to one side where he could see the two men.

"You're the one I had in mind," Frank said, his voice edged with suspicion. "Have you been playing around up in the barn loft?"

"You askin' the boy if he's been prayin' in the barn loft?" Sol inquired, his voice rising to a whine. "No business of yours where he prays."

"No, Dad. Frank asked if Teddy had been *playing* in the loft," Vic explained.

"The boy's been in the house with me," Sol declared. He turned then, shuffling back to the kitchen, pushing Teddy on ahead toward the living room. "Go on now, like I told you. You can watch television until your father comes. Will keep you out from underfoot."

Teddy looked up, his eyes wide with hurt at Sol's gruffness. With his back to Frank and Vic, Sol winked at the boy. Suppressing a smile, Teddy went on into the other room.

"As I said, Frank came over earlier," Vic was explaining, "to check on his things. Seems someone tried to break into one of the crates. He thought maybe the boy got curious."

Ignoring the remark, Sol commented, "I was up in the loft this mornin'. Had to push some hay down for the horses." He turned, looking directly at Frank. "Noticed one of your crates cracked open. You must have banged it real good when you and Vic hoisted it up there. If you got clothes or such inside, you might have trouble with mice now that they can find their way in."

"Dad, you stay down from the loft! You've got no business up there anymore, now that the cattle are gone. Let Ted take care of his own horses." Then in a more resigned tone, "Besides, I was just telling you about that crate. Weren't you listening?"

Sol turned vacant eyes to his son. "You were tellin' me about what?"

Vic shook his head, glancing at Frank. "I suppose we could have smashed it. We did have trouble with one of them."

Frank's jaw line tightened. "Maybe."

"Come on." Vic headed for the door. "We'd better see if we can fix it. There are some old boards laying around we can use."

"Never mind." Frank reached out to stop Vic. "There's really nothing in that one to worry about. I'll come back tomorrow to take care of it while you and Nina are in town Christmas shopping." He looked at his watch. "Which reminds me, we'd better get back. She said she'd have dinner ready soon."

As Vic and Frank were walking toward the car, Ted drove in. Teddy followed Sol outside. "Mom and Kathy are with him," the boy remarked.

Sol had met May Bowen already, but not their teen-age daughter. Vic stopped to speak to Ted as the woman and girl got out of Ted's car. Sol nodded in May's direction as he and Teddy walked up behind Vic and Frank.

"How are the horses getting along?" Vic inquired.

"Just fine. Going to try driving them one of these days, as soon as. . . ." Ted hesitated, glancing at Sol, who was shaking his head. "As soon as I can put the harness together and locate a wagon."

Vic glanced at his father. "Remember now, I want you to stay out of that car."

Sol's shoulders drooped. "What was that? You sayin' I should stay out of the cold?"

Moving closer, Vic raised his voice, emphasizing each word. "I said, I-don't-want-you-driving-your-car!"

"Sure," Sol said with a shrug. "You can borrow my

car anytime I'm not usin' it."

Vic turned away, muttering. "Seems you hear things you want to just fine." He glanced at Ted. "Other times he can't understand a word."

"You'll have to speak up." Sol was nearly shouting. "What'd you say?"

"Oh, come on," Frank urged, leading the way to Vic's car.

Ted edged closer to Sol as the two men walked away. Lowering his voice he noted, "I hope Teddy hasn't been bothering you."

"He's not the one who's a bother."

"I don't believe you've met our daughter Kathy."

Sol turned toward the tall, blond teenager in jeans and purple sweatshirt. The girl glanced at her mother whispering, "I sure hope *I* don't get like that when I'm old."

Slowly Sol stood erect. The girl's face flushed as he looked at her, realizing he had heard. "I thought—I mean, I thought he couldn't hear. He couldn't just a minute ago."

"Sol usually hears just fine, Kathy," Ted rebuked. "Perhaps you should think through your opinions before mouthing them next time."

"But. . . ." The girl turned away. "That other man was shouting and still he couldn't hear."

Ted smiled. "I know. I don't quite understand what Sol's up to. For some reason he doesn't want his son knowing he's fully in charge of his senses." Ted looked at Sol. "What kind of game *are* you playing, anyway?"

Kathy's embarrassment was evident as she stared down at her sneaker-clad feet.

"It's all right," Sol spoke to the girl. "When I was your age I didn't think I'd ever be old either. Lately, though, I'm seein' age as only a slowin' of the body. In Vic's mind I'm past being of worth. Used to feel that way about myself until your dad came along with his horses." Sol glanced at Ted. "Wonder if you have any idea how long it's been since anyone cared what I thought, or wanted my advice?"

Kathy remained stolid as Sol followed Ted and his family to the barn. May fell behind to walk with Sol, her manner betraying her own embarrassment over her daughter's blunder. "How long have you lived here, Sol?"

"Born here." He glanced at her. She was short and a little plump. Seemed pleasant enough. He put his hand on her arm, lowering his voice. "Don't worry none about what the girl said."

She sighed, then smiled in evident relief.

Mike snorted when Ted opened the side door to let the horses in the barn. Bell went right to her stall, reaching out her long heavy head for a jaw rub from Sol.

"I like hearing them chew," Teddy said, pulling himself up to sit atop the manger as his father pitched in the hay he had pushed down earlier. "You know, Dad, draft horses are a lot different than saddle horses. Almost like a different kind of animal."

"That's silly," Kathy said, breaking her silence. "A horse is a horse. These are just bigger than the ones we used to have, that's all."

"I don't know," her father remarked. "I can't explain it, but there does seem to be a difference. Mike's as snorty as that big red saddle gelding we had back in Iowa, but there *is* something that sets him apart. What do you suppose it is, Sol?"

Sol gave Bell a final pat. "I never had much to do with saddle horses. But there seems to be something more dependable about a workhorse. Even ones like Mike here who tend to be a bit high-strung. They may jerk you around, but for the most part they seem to want to do what you ask of 'em."

"The kids at school think horses are dumb," Kathy spoke up.

"I don't believe any of us care about your school friends' opinions," her mother admonished. "Why on earth are you out of sorts this evening?" May looked at Sol. "Kathy feels she's out grown horses and thinks her father and brother should, too. She was hoping we'd invest the money from the sale of our saddle horses on something more practical. Like another car."

Sol controlled an urge to tease the girl. "Kathy, don't run horses down. The good Lord must have taken special pleasure in creatin' them. You've got to admit," he gestured toward the blacks, "they're beautiful creatures."

"I don't believe in all that creation stuff anymore," Kathy responded.

Sol shook his head. "You'll never convince me those two evolved from the sea or wherever it is you seem to think we all came from. Takes more imagination to believe that than what the Bible says happened in the beginning."

Fidgeting, May noted, "Ted, shouldn't we be going home. It's nearly dinnertime."

As the Bowens were leaving, Teddy hung back, whispering to Sol, "What we gonna do about those guns up there?"

"We'll talk about it later," Sol said, cautioning Teddy to lower his voice. "Need to keep it our secret for now. Wouldn't want the youngsters around here findin' we've got guns in the barn."

Teddy's eyes widened. "I hadn't thought of that! I won't tell anyone. I promise!"

After Sol's supper was over, Vic returned alone to find his father in the living room, the television keeping him company as usual. Vic turned the volume down, sitting on the edge of a nearby chair.

Sol could tell something was on Vic's mind. "Now what you want?" he demanded.

"Dad. . . ." Vic seemed subdued by his father's tone. "You make it sound as though I'm always badgering you. I'm just trying to see you're taken care of. I know I neglected you when Mom died."

"You didn't even remember the anniversary of her death a few weeks ago," his father accused.

"I remembered. I didn't want to remind you in case you'd forgotten."

"What do you mean? I'll never forget that day!"

Vic sighed. "You do forget things. Like," he pulled an envelope from his pocket and opened it, "this. It's from the tax collector's office. It came today. I didn't look at my mail until a little while ago. Do you realize you're behind in your property taxes?"

Sol squinted at the envelope Vic held out to him. "Couldn't be. Always pay 'em as soon as they're due."

"Well, you didn't pay this one. You're over a year behind. You haven't paid a cent since before Mom died." Vic's tone became accusing. "Someone at their office must have known I was back and sent this notice to my attention."

"How come they didn't send it to me?" Sol demanded. "Got no letter sayin' my taxes were overdue."

"Seems they've sent you an overdue notice but received no response."

"Never got no letter from 'em," Sol repeated.

"Dad, there are days you don't even walk down to

get your mail. And when you do I find half of it un-opened in the garbage. The kids have nearly demol-ished your mailbox. There's no door on it any longer. Things could be blown out and washed away in the ditch."

Vic leaned back, cooling to a less abrasive tone. "We can take care of the taxes and penalty with no trouble. But it brings up the question of whether you should continue living here alone like this. You've been a little better lately about cooking for yourself. But I don't like you starting to drive again. Now there's this tax thing." He sighed. "I really don't know what to do about you."

Sol eyed his son through half-closed lids. "Just what you gettin' at?"

"Frank and I have been talking. His idea about building a shopping center on that field of yours is a pretty good one. It would bring in a sizable chunk. You could live in luxury at that new retirement home they're building on the other side of town. You'd have your own apartment, three meals a day, and be with people your own age. They're planning to take bus trips and. . . ." Vic stopped when he saw his father had closed him off. "Dad, are you listening?"

Sol leaned forward. "You're voice seems to be fadin'. What was that you said about a bus trip? You takin' Frank along are you?"

Sighing again, Vic stood up, placing a hand on his father's shoulder. "No, Dad. We'll talk about this again some other time." He moved across the room. "I'll leave this tax bill on the kitchen table. Be back in the morning to help write the check." He stopped in the doorway looking back at his father.

Turning in his chair, Sol watched his son walk to-ward the kitchen. "Vic."

"Yes, Dad?" The younger man stopped.

"Are you tryin' to pitch me off my own land? Is that what this is all about?"

"No." Vic was shaking his head. "It's just that I don't know what to do about you, for you, any longer. I've tried everything, but. . . ." He held out his hands, letting them fall helplessly to his side. "I'll see you in the morning."

With that Vic turned and left. Sol sat there listening to the back door open and close. Alone again, he felt the walls closing in around him—the same walls that had witnessed his first faltering steps as a child, his teen years, Ruth coming here with him as his wife, their children's growing-up years. What was happening to him? He thought he was getting a handle on himself, helping Ted with the horses and all. He enjoyed having Teddy around. He was taking complete care of his own needs now that Frank had come to take up Vic's time. So how had a bill for his taxes gone unpaid? How could that have happened? He'd always paid his bills on time. Always! He might have forgotten awhile back when he hadn't been himself, but he would certainly have known if an unpaid notice had come lately.

At last Sol pulled himself to his feet and walked to the kitchen. He stood by the table fingering Vic's letter from the tax collector's office. Sol raised his head, his eyes closed as he steadied himself with a hand on the back of a chair. "My Friend, why? Why is this happening to me? Just when I thought I was puttin' my life back together after Ruth's passing. How could I have missed payin' my taxes? I haven't been that far gone. Or have I?"

After standing there for some time Sol went to the bedroom, coming back with his checkbook, an envelope, and a stamp. He sat down and wrote a check to cover the taxes as well as the penalty. At the bottom he wrote "Sorry" before placing the sealed envelope on the table.

"Have to go in to the bank tomorrow to transfer funds. Vic can drive me. Maybe he's right. Maybe I shouldn't be trusted with the car. Or anything else, for that matter." With that, Sol turned off the lights and went to bed. It had been a long day. A very long day.

Morning came after a fitful night of dreams. In one he was being chased by a fat dog strangely resembling Frank. The December sun slanted in through his bedroom window, prying Sol's eyes open. He was nearly as tired as when he had come to bed the night before.

He dressed and went out to the kitchen. The letters, the one Vic had brought over the night before and the one with the check he had written, lay on the table. That had been no dream. Was he incapable of caring for himself? The question was depressing.

Just as Sol was about to put the coffeepot on the stove, he heard Vic drive up. He was still standing by the sink when his son came in the house. "You really should keep your back door locked at night, Dad. It's not safe these days leaving your house unlocked."

Sol shrugged. "Forgot, I guess."

"Have you eaten breakfast?"

"Was about to."

"Sit down. I'll get it for you." Vic took the coffeepot from his father and put it on the stove to heat.

The older man moved to the table where he wearily sank to a chair, tapping the envelope with the check he had written the night before. "There's a check in here for the taxes. It's ready to mail. If you want to drive me to the bank this mornin' I'll transfer money from my savings to cover it."

Vic nodded as he broke an egg into the sputtering frying pan. "I did a lot of thinking after I was here last night." He dropped a slice of bread in the toaster. "Why don't we go to a lawyer this morning and have a power of attorney drawn up in my name. That way I'll be able to handle things like this for you so you won't have to worry about it. You'll be able to relax and take it easy."

Sol stared Vic's back. "Another of Frank's ideas?"

Vic turned. "Frank mentioned it. But it's been on my mind, too."

Feeling beaten, Sol shook his head. "I'll have to think on it."

"We could get something started today, if you'd like," Vic suggested. "It shouldn't take long."

7

World A-Crumble

Sol shook his head. "Not today. Not ready even to think about it."

Vic set a plate of eggs and toast in front of his father, then prowled the kitchen while Sol ate, opening cupboard doors and examining hinges. "This place does need a lot of work."

Ignoring Vic's pointed remark, Sol bent over the breakfast before him with determination. He wanted to get this trip to town over and done.

By the time the bank opened, Sol and Vic were parked in front of the low brick building. It did not take long to transfer funds from Sol's savings to checking. He couldn't help thinking about his own father during the transaction. The man would never have believed the sum Sol had on deposit from the sale of his land to those developers. He was also positive his father would not have approved.

But what was he to do? Vic showed no interest in the farm. He had made more money in the Middle East oil fields than Sol had in a lifetime on the land. The money from the sale of his property meant nothing to Sol now. It would remain in the bank collecting interest until he was gone, finally divided between his neglectful daughter and overbearing son. It was strange the way things worked out, he decided, as he walked out of the bank with Vic. While farming he barely had enough to make one end meet the other. Now, with the land, cows, and Ruth gone, he had more than he needed or cared to use.

As he got into the car Vic again brought up the subject of a power of attorney. "Are you sure you don't want me to take over these things for you, Dad?"

"Not sure about anything right now," Sol admitted. "Just want to go back home and rest. Didn't get much sleep last night."

Vic drove Sol back to the farm in silence, stopping at the back steps to let his father out. Opening the car door, Sol struggled to get free of the small, cramped vehicle. "Guess I'd better feed Jake, then get myself some breakfast before takin' a rest. You go on home. I can manage."

"Dad!" Vic was leaning across the seat toward him. "You've already had breakfast. I cooked it for you before we went to town. Remember?"

"Sure. I know that!" Sol declared, his mind trying to untangle his thoughts. "Was talkin' about old Jake. Got to go fix *his* breakfast." He slammed the car door hard, heading for the house, stumbling as he reached the steps. He caught himself, grabbing the handrail before starting on up.

"We've got to talk about that power of attorney, Dad," Vic called. "And soon!"

Sol ignored the remark as he went on inside without turning to look at his son. He leaned back against the closed door, listening as the car turned and headed off down the driveway. "Have I gone clear off, my Friend? Gone plum screwy? Forgot all about that egg Vic cooked for me earlier. Then had to go and let him know I forgot. Not too smart. Nope. Not smart at all!"

Clouds had moved in, completely blocking the anemic winter sun. It smelled of rain again. But Sol cared nothing about the weather. How could he care about anything with his sanity slipping from him. He longed only to ease himself down on the living-room couch and go to sleep, escaping his fears and problems. But there was Jake. Someone had to take care of the dog.

"Would a power of attorney see to old Jake's needs, too?" Sol wondered aloud as he scraped some leftovers into the dog's dish to carry to the barn. He sighed. He hadn't felt this washed-out in weeks.

As he pushed the barn door open, Mike and Bell nickered expectantly. Sol stopped short, Jake's dish in his hand. He had forgotten all about the horses. They should have been turned out hours ago. Sol felt sick clear to the pit of his stomach. He would have to talk to Ted. Tell him to stop by in the mornings after this to take care of the horses himself.

Sol stood there berating himself as the dog laboriously pulled himself to his feet. Man and dog greeted each other without a sound or touch. There was no need. The one well understood the other's frailties.

After feeding the horses and turning them into the pasture, Sol went out through the side door to check on the water tank. It was nearly full. He was walking toward the small gate by the corner of the barn when someone called to him.

"Morning." It was Frank.

Seeing no car, Sol figured the man must have walked across the field from Vic's place.

Frank stood there, elbows on the gate top just looking at him. "Vic said you wanted to talk to me. Is it about those crates of mine?"

Sol stopped, reaching for the gate latch. "Told Vic

no such thing. Your name never even came up this mornin'."

"Are you sure? Try thinking a little harder. Didn't you want to ask me something?"

"No need thinkin' harder. Never talked about you or those crates." Had he said something to Vic about Frank? Sol wondered. He couldn't remember.

Frank stepped back as Sol opened the gate. The man seemed to be waiting for him to work it all out in his mind. Sol glared at him. The more he saw of this pompous, puffy-soft man, the less there was to like. But then, Sol admitted to himself, there was a whole lot of people he'd come to dislike during the past year, including those city folk and their kids taking roost all over the place, poking into things, messing up the landscape.

"What's the matter, Sol? Forget what it was you wanted to talk to me about?"

There was a jarring ring to Frank's words. It struck Sol this was the first time the man had used his given name. At least he didn't call him Dad or Pops. Sol didn't think he could handle that.

Shaking his head, Sol noted, "Don't recall mentionin' a thing to Vic. But since you're here—I saw what looked to be rifles inside one of those crates of yours. The one that's broke open. A barn loft don't hardly seem the place to store guns. Too many kids pokin' around. If they ever got hold of them there could be trouble to pay!"

"I had a feeling it was that Bowen kid who broke into the crate. What's his name? Teddy?"

Sol shook his head. "Wasn't Teddy. He's okay."

"Then maybe it was an older kid."

"Who you aimin' at?"

"You."

88

"Nope. Weren't me tore into it either. Looked in after I saw it broke open. But that was all." Sol was mad now. How dare Frank call him a kid. "Where'd you get those guns?"

"None of your business!" Frank snapped. He stopped, a forced smile settling weak and puny across his wide face. "They were given to me when my last wife and I divorced. They were part of the settlement."

"Your *last* wife? Had more than one, have you?"

The flesh around Frank's sunken eyes turned rage-red, as he struggled to maintain an outward calm. "I married for the second time after returning from the Middle East. But it didn't work. For either of us. We broke up shortly before I came here."

"I still say keepin' a bunch of guns in a damp barn isn't the most intelligent idea anyone ever came up with," Sol noted. "Especially with kids so close, nosin' around into everything."

With that said, Sol headed for the house. For some reason this little set-to with Frank had buoyed his spirits, sharpening his mind. While he felt some better, he was still bone-tired. When he reached the house he turned to look back along the path to the barn. Frank was nowhere in sight. Evidently he had gone back to Vic's place.

A raindrop flattened on the back of his hand as he opened the door. "Aw, well," he muttered, "might be kinda nice takin' a nap with the rain rattlin' against the window glass."

Noon came and went with Sol stretched out on the living-room couch, his stockinged feet covered with a green afghan Ruth had knit. Outside the rain continued to fall, wetting down the last of the brown leaves under the oak trees.

It was three o'clock when he awoke. He was hungry. It had been hours since the egg-and-toast breakfast Vic cooked for him. Sol sat up. He was feeling around with his toes for his slippers when a knock thundered on the back door. Couldn't be Vic, Sol reasoned. He would have come on in. Padding out through the kitchen he found Teddy standing at the back door dripping wet.

"The pasture gate was wide-open by the corner of the barn," the boy blurted out as Sol stepped back to let him in. The boy's blond hair was rain-matted to his head, his eyes wild. "I closed it. The horses hadn't found it yet. At least they didn't get out. But they could have! It wasn't me who left the gate open, Sol. Honest. I hardly ever go through there."

Sol stood dazed, his mind still half asleep, his hand gripping the door knob as Teddy dripped on across the porch floor to the kitchen. Had *he* left the gate open after talking to Frank? Sol wondered, with a jab of guilt. He thought he remembered closing it. And yet—he had been forgetting things lately.

"As long as there's no harm done," Sol remarked, trying to dismiss the matter as he followed Teddy into the kitchen. And yet deep inside he was wondering. Could he trust himself any longer? Guilt took a large bite of his conscience as he motioned Teddy toward a chair by the table.

"Are you okay?" Teddy asked. "You don't look so good."

Sol sat down. "It's just that I—I may have been the one who left the gate open. I came through there earlier when Frank was over. I was sure I'd closed it. Almost positive."

"Maybe that guy Frank left it open. I don't like him much."

"I don't know, boy. I don't like him either, but I've got to admit, I've been forgettin' a whole lot of things lately. Just found I forgot to pay my property taxes. Must have been gettin' letters from the tax collector's office right along. Threw 'em away, I expect. Don't rightly recall. Now my taxes are way past due and Vic's after me to sign away my right to take care of myself. Thinks I should turn everything over to him, make out a paper givin' him power to run everything for me."

Teddy slid over onto a chair next to the older man, touching Sol's gnarled hand. "Don't let him do that to you, Sol. You can still do lots of things."

Sol turned his head to look at the boy, tears brimming his eyes. "I don't know, Teddy. I just don't know anymore. Maybe I *am* ready for the old folks' home. That's where Vic would like to ship me."

"You can't go there!" Teddy insisted. "Maybe the letters fell out of your mailbox. Or maybe somebody took them."

"Who'd want 'em? No. Lately I've been doin' some pretty strange things."

"No you haven't, Sol. You've been helping Dad with the horses. You've done all the work on the harness. You know lots more about draft horses than we do. Dad said so."

Sol smiled mechanically, but no sparkle was in his eyes. His head was beginning to ache. Then he remembered, he hadn't eaten lunch. "You hungry, boy? How about a peanut-butter sandwich?"

"Yah. I am kinda hungry."

"Why don't you fix one for each of us. You know where the bread and things are, don't you?"

Teddy started to get up, then stopped. "Maybe you'd better do it. I always tear the bread when I try to spread peanut butter. But I'll help."

When the sandwiches were ready the two sat back at the table again. Teddy was smiling. "See, Sol. You can still do anything you want to. You don't have to go to one of them old people's places."

As Teddy was leaving later, Sol asked him to tell his father he'd better stop by in the mornings on his way to work to take care of the horses. "Tell him I'm not feelin' up to lookin' after 'em anymore."

Reluctantly, Teddy agreed.

Sol was standing in the open doorway watching the boy walk down the steps when Ted drove up to the barn. Stepping back inside he closed the door, heading for the bedroom, turning off the lights in the kitchen and living room as he went. He didn't want to see anyone right then. If Ted saw the lights were on he might come to the house when Teddy gave him the message.

The peanut-butter sandwich and milk had taken the edge off Sol's hunger. Skipping dinner, he was in bed before dark, escaping his confusion in sleep. Sometime during the night he awoke, lying there wondering if he had turned the lock on the back door. That question kept him awake until at last he got up. Switching on the bedside lamp, then the overhead living room light, Sol made his way through the darkened kitchen and onto the porch.

"That was a useless trip," he muttered to himself as he tried the outside door to find it locked tight. He had, however, neglected to close the door between the porch and kitchen. Not that it really mattered, except that he usually shut it at night. He closed the door, then after a side trip to the bathroom, Sol went back to his bed, where he was soon asleep once again.

Morning found him feeling rested and some better. And yet the dread of rising to face another day—if it was to be anything like the past two—was more than he cared to contemplate. At last he talked himself out of bed and slowly pulled on his clothes, catching sight of his Bible as he dressed. He hadn't even opened it lately.

"Should do that," he decided, "later on. Haven't been talkin' to you as much either, my Friend."

Sol sighed. Nothing, just nothing, seemed right. As he padded toward the kitchen in his slippers, he glanced at the wet rivulets coursing down the living room windows. It was still raining.

He stopped abruptly. Something was wrong. The kitchen light was on. "Must have forgotten it when I got up durin' the night."

But, no! He remembered making his way through the darkened kitchen by the light from the living room. He stepped on into the room, stopping again. There, in the middle of the floor, was Jake's dish heaped with raw hamburger topped with an egg, its single yellow eye staring up at him. He distinctly remembered carrying Jake's dish to the barn the day before. He hadn't brought it back. Teddy didn't have it when he came to the house the evening before. It had *not* been on the floor when he came out during the night to check the lock on the back door. If the dish had been there, he would have tripped over it.

But that was not all that was wrong. The refrigerator door was standing open. Splattered inside was a second egg, its smashed shell strung over a bottom shelf.

Sol shuffled around the dog's dish to close the refrigerator as questions tumbled through his mind. Had he gone back out to the barn without remembering, bringing Jake's dish in, filling it, then leaving the refrigerator open and the kitchen light burning?

Could he have done all that with absolutely no memory of it? Even for a worthless old fool like himself, it seemed impossible, he decided, as the pain and confusion of past days flooded in to nearly suffocate him. What was happening to him?

He stood there going over the things he could recall. He had come out to check the lock on the door. "I remember doin' that," Sol said aloud. "The door to the porch was open and I closed it." He glanced up. The door was still closed as he had left it.

Crossing the room Sol tried to open it, but the button lock on the handle had been pushed in, locking it tight. He seldom locked that door. Opening it, Sol went out to try the outside door. It was still locked, as he had found it during the night. He flipped the lever.

"My Friend," Sol whispered prayerfully, "help me find some sense in this. Please!" His usual conversation with his God and Friend turned to desperation. Nothing made sense anymore. Absolutely nothing.

Numbed, shuffling his feet, he turned back to the kitchen. From habit he put the coffeepot on to heat before picking up Jake's full dish, carrying it out to the back step. If the dog got hungry he would probably come to the house on his own and find it there. Sol was not up to making a trip to the barn.

The wintry weather was typical of western Oregon, dark and dismal, and so Sol left the kitchen light ablaze as he sat hunched over his cup at the table. If he could only piece the last few hours together. Something had happened. But what? It appeared he could not handle the simplest tasks any longer. "Should be locked in a loony tank," he said aloud, drawing some comfort from the sound of his own voice.

An hour passed. Sol's half cup of coffee cooled. Still

he sat there, his elbows braced on the tabletop. He was past the point of thinking now. Nothing meshed. Nothing fit. He was so submerged in his misery he did not even hear the footfalls on the backporch steps until the door opened and closed.

"Dad?"

Sol remained silent.

"Oh, there you are. I thought you might be at the barn. Can I do anything for you before Frank and I go to town?"

Raising his head Sol noticed Frank standing behind Vic, a smile stretching across his wide face. Sol closed his eyes. But when he opened them the two men were still there looking down at him.

"You might take Jake's breakfast out to him if he hasn't already come to the house. I put his dish outside by the door." Looking into Vic's face then, Sol asked—fearful of the reply, "It *was* on the top step, wasn't it?"

Vic nodded. "I'll take it out to him. Should I turn Ted's horses loose, too?"

"You can if they're still in the barn. But I figure Ted probably came by earlier to see to them."

"Are you all right, Dad?" Vic inquired. "You're not sick are you?"

Sol shook his head. "I'm fine. Just fine."

"I'll stay with him while you go to the barn," Frank offered.

"Don't need no nursemaid!" Sol blustered.

"I'd appreciate it," Vic said, ignoring Sol's protest as he went out the door.

Frank poured himself a cup of coffee without being invited. "Want yours heated up?"

Sol started to decline, then changed his mind, pushing his cup toward the edge of the table.

"Vic told me he thinks it's time you moved to a retirement home." Frank's well-oiled words cut through Sol's gloom. "Have you given it any thought?" He pulled a chair out, sitting across the table from the older man.

Taking a sip of the now over-stout black brew, Sol allowed the question to slide over him without reply.

"You know," Frank was going on, "I put my mother in a retirement home a few years back. She was positive she wasn't going to like it. She fought going for months until she nearly burned the house down around her when she left a stove burner on. Couldn't even remember turning it on. But, you know, once she moved to the home she found she really liked it. Said she wished she'd gone years before. I'll bet you'd like it, too."

"Not used to bein' around folks all the time," Sol remarked.

"Vic tells me this new place in town has apartments where you can live by yourself if you want to."

"I'm by myself here—at least most of the time." Sol eyed the man, hoping he'd take the hint.

"You'd get three meals a day. There'd be other people to talk to if you wanted company." Frank stopped, then added, "It hasn't been easy on Vic, worrying about you over here all alone, not knowing what's going on or how you are."

Sol sighed. "Just the thought of packin' and movin' takes more energy than I've got right now."

"That's okay," Frank noted, his voice low and coaxing. "All you'll need is to sign over a power of attorney to Vic, pack a few clothes, and go. I'll help with the furniture you want to take along."

Staring at him, Sol wondered if perhaps Frank might be right. While he didn't think much of the man, it could be Frank was on target for once.

Vic came back into the house at that moment. "The horses had already been turned out. Ted must have been over earlier. They are his animals, after all. No reason you should have to take care of them."

"I like doin' it. Most of the time, anyway." Sol sat there ramrod straight, looking at his son. Maybe he *should* turn things over to Vic. Just let go. Give in.

"Vic," Sol began, swallowing nothing down his dry throat. "I guess it's time."

"Time?" Vic questioned. "Time for what?"

"Time I signed that power of attorney over to you. The one you been talkin' about. If you still want to take care of things for me, that is."

8

You're Going to Do What?

It was midafternoon when Vic drove his father home, the newly signed power of attorney between them on the dash. Sol wondered if he was supposed to feel relieved. Wasn't that what this was all about—the turning of his rights and responsibilities over to his son? Instead, he felt wrung out, drained, his independence dead and drying. The only thing missing was the plaintive wail of a burial dirge.

Vic drove on home, where Nina and Frank waited as Sol walked up the steps to the house alone. In the living room he pulled the gold draperies partly closed—draperies he'd helped Ruth hang shortly before her death. He stood looking out through the narrow opening for a few minutes. The rain had not let up, falling from a heavy water-laden sky. Here he was again, in the house where he began life as a newborn, once more dependent—dependent now upon his own son. A son who knew nothing of the inner feelings of the man who had fathered him.

Sol sought his favorite overstuffed chair, wearily lowering himself into its comfort. A sudden longing engulfed him. Oh, for human arms to encircle him once more, for someone to hold him. He leaned his head back against the worn upholstery, staring at the wood molding bordering the wall just below the ceiling.

"Lord. My good Friend. You're so far away. So far. . . ."

A sob wrenched his body, welling up from somewhere deep inside. He had never felt this alone in his entire life. Not even after Ruth's death, and that had been the meanest blow he'd faced up to then. But this! This was an end to everything. He had thought that would come only after his own death, not while he was still living and breathing. Losing the ability to be his own man was worse than death.

Tears boiled over, dampening his line-creased face as he struggled to hold himself together. "Please, Lord!" his voice croaked. "Please help me! Please. . . ."

But there was nothing. No comforting sensation. No strong sense of God's presence. Nothing.

After some minutes Sol pulled a handkerchief from his pocket and mopped at his face. While he felt no better, there was at least a release of the festering tension that had been building. And yet there was still no inner peace, no sureness of God's presence.

"Lord," he began, wadding the white square of cloth and stuffing it back in his overall pocket, "have I been believin' a myth all these years? Are you only an imagined Being? Is that all my life's Friend has ever been?"

He felt no guilt in voicing his doubts, his griefs, his disappointments. In times past he would have expected to be struck dead if he had thought such things.

"How could I have done these things and not remember?" He shook his fist at the ceiling. "Look at me! Here I am talkin' to you still. And I'm not even sure there is a you. But if you *don't* exist. . . ."

He could not bring himself to consider that possibility. If his longtime Friend had never existed—if there were no God—his whole life had been without purpose, a wasted effort now near its end.

"If you *are* there, Lord, if you *do* hear, if you *are* real, please do something! Let me know. Send some kind of sign. I can't go on like this. I don't know what to do, or how to do it. I've hit bottom, Lord. And I don't even know how to die."

Sol closed his eyes. The only sound in the room was that of his own breathing. How he longed for even that to stop. Maybe he should do something to make it stop! Maybe he should!

Time passed. Minutes. Or was it hours? There was no way of knowing. For Sol, time compressed into a godless eternity as he sat embraced by his old chair, sheltered within the house that had been his world. He had no desire to move or even open his eyes. Maybe he would just sit there and rot. Rot away, slipping off into nothingness.

The rattle of a doorknob finally nudged his consciousness back to reality.

"Sol? You home?"

Pulled from the pit where he had been mired, Sol opened his eyes. It wasn't Vic or Frank. It wasn't even Ted. It certainly wasn't Teddy. Could it be? No! Not God. He didn't need to open doors. Sol shook his head. Now he was positive he was losing his grip on reality.

Someone was walking through the kitchen, coming toward the living room.

"I looked for you at the barn. Figured you must be in here when I didn't see you outside. Say, are you all right?"

Sol turned his head toward the voice. It was Perry.

"Fine. Just fine."

Coming into the room, Perry stood looking down at his former neighbor. "No, you're not fine, Solomon Timins. I can see that for myself. Mind if I sit awhile?"

Sol shrugged.

"You sick or something?" the man questioned, easing himself down on the couch.

Sol shook his head.

"Then what's the matter? Or am I too nosy?"

After staring at Perry for a moment, Sol at last remarked, "You're lookin' at a defeated, empty old man, Perry. One who's lived a useless, needless existence. Not even capable of takin' care of himself anymore."

Concern veiled Perry's face. "What's happened? You were full of plans for those horses you and that fella Ted bought last time we talked."

Taking a deep breath, Sol began at the beginning, highlighting the last couple days: from the unpaid taxes to the newly witnessed power of attorney. Perry leaned forward intently when Sol got to the part about finding the kitchen light on and Jake's dish on the floor that morning.

"There has to be an explanation," the man offered. "You're not *that* loony, Sol."

A smile tugged the corners of Sol's mouth. Although God had seldom been mentioned between them, Sol had never known Perry as a believer. Should he tell him, he wondered, of his doubts about God? No, he decided. Better not.

Perry was sitting on the edge of the couch staring down at his hands, elbows braced on his knees. At last he raised his shaggy gray head. "Sol, what's happened to your faith? What's happened to the man I've watched for forty some years? The man who never walked a step without God beside him?"

Disbelieving what he'd heard, Sol questioned, "How— how'd you know? I never talked about it much."

Perry's eyes drilled him through. "No, you didn't.

And you seldom went to church. I always wondered about that. I know since Vera and I been going it's helped us steer a lot straighter course."

That was a surprise. Sol hadn't known Perry and Vera had started going to church. Looking away, Sol nodded. "I guess maybe I've been wrong. Not only for Ruth and my kids' sake, but for my own. Thought I could handle things just fine by myself." He looked up. "Suppose it's been nothin' more than pride, thinkin' I didn't need anyone or anything."

"Could be," Perry agreed. "It was pride, you know, caused the first man and woman's downfall in the very beginning."

"Do you remember the time we were looking over our places after that freak tornado ripped through here, damaging my barn and destroying our hay crops? I was mad as a teased hornet. But you just smiled, reminding me how we were all still alive. You said—and I'll never forget—what God gave wasn't ours to start with, so we hadn't really lost a thing. As for you, you said you planned to continue walking on with him no matter what came your way."

"I said that?"

Perry nodded. "You did."

Sol rubbed his cheek with the back of a thumb. "I don't recall."

"It was little seeds like that, planted in my mind, got me to thinking seriously about God. So don't you let me or him down now. You hang on, Sol. Loosen up on the reins a little. Give him a chance to work things out for you."

"I think maybe the Lord sent you to me today," Sol noted with some relief.

Before Perry could reply, a banging came from the back of the house.

"Someone's knocking on your door," Perry said. "Want me to see who it is?"

Sol nodded.

When Perry returned, Teddy was with him, ruddy of face and out of breath.

"I've got something for you, Sol!" the boy gasped. "Look!" He was pulling soiled, wrinkled envelopes out of a pocket. One dropped to the floor.

Perry stooped to pick it up, brushing at the dirt. He glanced at the address. "It's yours, Sol. And look who it's from. The tax collector."

Sol reached for the letter as Teddy dumped several more damp envelopes onto his lap. He looked at the postmarks. The one Perry had picked up was dated in May of the year before. "Where'd you get these?" Sol asked.

"One of the guys was talking awhile back about some letters he'd taken from a mailbox. I didn't know they were yours. Marty—he's older than the rest of us—warned the other kid he could get in real big trouble with the government, maybe even be put in prison, for fooling around with someone else's mail. The guy who did it said the mail from that box was hardly ever picked up. He figured no one cared much. Anyway, he said he hadn't opened it. He got real scared when he found out the FBI could come looking for him, so he stashed it all in a hollow tree. The rest of us stayed clear of the place so no one would think we had anything to do with it if it was ever found."

"You mean my mail's been in a tree all this time?" Sol questioned.

Teddy nodded. "I got to thinking maybe it was yours after you told me about not getting those letters from the tax place. So I went to the tree right after school today and there they were. All of 'em have your name on the front. So, you see, Sol, you didn't forget to pay your taxes after all. You just didn't get the letters."

Shuffling through the envelopes, Sol could see Teddy was right. Three were from the tax collector's office. Several others were addressed to occupant. There was one advertising a prepaid funeral plan, and a couple store circulars.

Perry was looking over Sol's shoulder. "The boy must have taken just what didn't seem important—to him, anyway. Or maybe," Perry chuckled, "he thought he was doing you a favor, taking the tax bills."

The sound of Perry's amusement brought Sol all the way back to reality as relief flooded him. He closed his eyes, sending off a brief thought-prayer of thanks.

"But what about all those other things?" he reminded Perry when he opened his eyes. "The dog dish on the floor? The open refrigerator? The locked door between the kitchen and porch? And what about Frank sayin' I wanted to talk to him when I couldn't remember wantin' to? And—" He glanced at Teddy. "There was that pasture gate left open, too."

"What's been going on?" Teddy questioned.

Briefly Sol filled the boy in on what had taken place the night before. Had it been only last night? It seemed years had passed since he had gotten out of bed that morning. When everything caved in on him.

"I don't know about that other stuff," Teddy remarked. "But I'll bet it was that guy Frank who left the gate open. Maybe he went through there when he walked back to your son's house. I don't think he likes you much, Sol. He sure doesn't like me!"

"He wouldn't have used that gate," Sol noted. "The barn lot's too muddy."

Perry, who had sat down again, leaned back

thoughtfully. Then he came alert and glanced up. "Wait a minute! Teddy may be onto something. Maybe Frank opened the gate after you came to the house so you would *think* you had left it open. Didn't you say he and Vic had both been trying to talk to you into signing that power of attorney?"

"Yes, but. . . ."

Teddy jumped in with, "Yeah, and he could have just made up that part about your son saying you wanted to talk to him!"

"Now why would the man want to do a thing like that?" Sol questioned.

Teddy sank down beside Perry. Side by side the boy and the man sat there staring at Sol.

"Are you tryin' to say you think Frank might have been helpin' Vic get hold of this place? I just can't believe. . . ." And yet past events came flooding back. Would Vic, his own son, really do such a thing to him?

"It is possible," Perry declared.

"But what about the dog dish on the kitchen floor, the open refrigerator, and the locked door to the porch? It wasn't like that when I got up to check on things last night. The outside door was locked tight, if you're thinkin' someone might have sneaked in when I went to bed earlier."

"Does Vic have a key?" Perry inquired.

Sol nodded. "But he wouldn't do anything like that. I mean, to his own father? We've never been close, but. . . ."

"Maybe it was Frank's idea," Teddy offered.

Perry picked up on the boy's reasoning. "That's possible. Frank may know where Vic keeps the key to your house. He could have come over in the night after you got up to check the door. Maybe he thought

105

he was doing Vic a favor, pushing you into that power of attorney."

Obviously enjoying being included in such an adult discussion, Teddy remarked, "We know *you* didn't do all that crazy stuff!"

Sol smiled. "We do? There's no way of provin' I didn't. Although I'd like to think it wasn't me. And yet, it leaves some unanswered questions hangin' in air. Until it's cleared up I'm gonna wonder if I might have walked in my sleep."

"Could be an explanation," Perry offered. "You've been pretty uptight lately."

"If I did walk in my sleep, out to the barn and back in the middle of the night, a judge would still declare me incompetent," Sol noted, thinking again of the power of attorney he had just signed over to Vic. Yes, there were a lot of things to straighten out.

Before Perry left, he invited Sol to go back to town with him for the night. But Sol knew he had to stay where he was. He had to find out for himself what was going on. He was sure of one thing at least, Jesus his Friend was real and still with him. Perry and Teddy coming just when they did, along with the letters Teddy brought, was all the proof Sol needed. The Lord had heard his cry, heard him beg for a sign, and had sent them to him. No one would ever be able to convince him otherwise.

The week eased by with Vic again coming over twice a day to check on his father. At least he never stayed long and Frank was seldom with him.

Pastor Brock stopped by one afternoon. Before he could invite Sol to church again, Sol surprised the minister by saying, "Been thinkin' about stopping by one of these Sunday mornin's."

Friday evening Sol went to the barn when Ted and

Teddy came by to take care of the horses. Ted showed relief at seeing him. "I've been trying to fit the harness on Mike and Bell, and I could sure use your help. I'll be bringing over an old hay wagon tomorrow. Found it stored in a barn on the other side of town. Got it real cheap. It's in fair shape. Was used behind a tractor for a few years, so I'll need to put a longer tongue on it."

"Be glad to help," Sol offered, feeling life seeping back to him after the confusion and despondency of the past week.

Perry called later that evening. Sol felt even closer to his former neighbor than before since learnings Perry had come to believe in Jesus. It gave Sol a more positive feeling about himself. His life *had* counted for something after all, if it led Perry to the Lord.

He enjoyed working with Ted again. The wagon Ted bought was in good shape. As they were trying to decide what to do for a wagon tongue, Sol remembered a long forgotten metal tongue stored on the wall ties under the rafters of his garage. Together, with Teddy giving them a hand, they lowered it to the ground, finding the metal rusty, but usable.

Later, Sol combed out Bell's tail while Teddy brushed her. The boy commented shyly, "It's fun having you work with us again. I missed you."

"I missed you and your dad, too," Sol admitted. "I'm feelin' a lot better than I was."

There had been no more forgetful lapses. No more doors or gates left unaccountably open or strangely locked. No more objects where they shouldn't be. Slowly Sol was recovering from the shock of it all. Even the power of attorney was not bothering him as much as at first. Since Vic never brought the subject up, Sol decided he would simply ignore the whole thing and go on about his life as before.

But the following Sunday, while watching the evening news cast on television, Sol was hit by an unexpected blow which dredged it all to the surface again where it could not be ignored. The local news commentator had been rambling on about a town council meeting. He then turned to a subject touching off sparks in Sol's brain.

A request to rezone a once-rural area just north of town, lately dominated by subdivisions, was also brought before the council today. Plans have been put forth to build a shopping mall on the last few acres that reamin of the old Timins dairy farm, one of the oldest farms left in the longtime farming community where only houses grow these days, side by side, front to back.

The council also considered—

But Sol heard no more. There was no need. Everything was lumping together into a solid, sickening mass. A shopping mall! On his land! Frank had been talking about a shopping mall. Vic had mentioned it, too. What was it Vic had suggested? Sell his land? Ship him off to a retirement home? Now that damnable power of attorney was beginning to make sense.

"So," Sol muttered to himself, "Perry and the boy were right. Frank and Vic are up to their necks in this." The hardest lump to swallow was Vic's part in it. Had his son set him up, with Frank's help, to get him to sign that power of attorney giving Vic control of everything?

Sol found it difficult to sleep that night. He had tried calling Vic on the phone time after time before going to bed. But the line was constantly busy. It was not a good sign, Sol decided.

The next morning he was washing dishes when the sound of voices filtered in from outside. Drying his hands, Sol went to back door, hoping Vic had come to explain. Maybe there had been a mistake. Maybe the news commentator had been wrong. But instead of Vic, Sol looked out to see three strangers between his house and barn. One was a man with a portable television camera perched on his shoulder. Another man, in a dark suit and tie, stood beside a woman dressed in heels and a bright red coat. She held a microphone to the suited man's face while the other pointed the camera at them.

9

Conspiracy

"Hey!" Sol yelled from the back door. "What's goin' on out here?"

Anger charged him like a mad bull. How dare they come onto his property without asking? "I said!" he demanded a second time, "what's goin' on out here?"

The three turned, the man with the camera angling the eye of the thing in Sol's direction.

"Mr. Timins?" the woman inquired as she minced toward him in spike heels never intended for a farm path. The man in the suit remained where he was, while the one with the camera followed the woman, keeping to one side so as to hold Sol in the viewfinder.

"Are you Solomon Timins?" she asked again.

"Who wants to know?" Sol snapped.

"We're from Station Twenty-Four, KUPB."

She had nearly reached the bottom step. Sol moved out onto the top platform to slow her progress. She wasn't getting in his house! He figured he knew why they were there.

"I'm Paula Rogers," the red-coated female said, holding the microphone with one hand as she extended the other toward him.

Sol knew who she was. He'd seen her on the tube. Ignoring the offered hand, he stood there glaring down at her, then at the cameraman beside her.

"Mr. Timins," the Rogers woman began, her free arm falling to her side, "how do you feel about your farm being surfaced over for a shopping mall?"

So there it was, laid out bare and open. The dread of the night before was now reality. "Who told you people you could come onto my property like this without askin'?" Sol demanded.

The woman ignored the question. "I understand your son, Victor Timins, will be building the mall."

"Got no son. Nobody by that name round here." Sol lied without a blink of an eye. "No mall's gonna be built on my place as long as I'm alive. Got no plans on checkin' out for quite a spell, either."

She appeared flustered. "Victor Timins has applied for a zone change. He noted on the application he holds power of attorney over his father, Solomon Timins." She hesitated, looking Sol square in the eye. "You *are* the elder Timins, aren't you? Solomon Timins?"

Sol stared at her, then finally nodded. In a clear, brittle voice he suggested, "I think it would be proper if you and those other two left." Lowering his voice, he added, "And right now!"

She started to say something more, then turned away. The three walked on down the driveway where Sol could see a couple cars parked along the roadside.

He sighed as he went back in the house. Picking up the telephone, he dialed Vic's number again. This time there was no busy signal.

"Hello."

He recognized Nina's voice. "Put Vic on," he demanded abruptly.

"Is that you, Father Timins?"

"It is."

"Vic's not here right now."

"You tell that son of mine the minute he gets back I want to talk to him." With that Sol hung up. He had no more than turned away from the phone when a faint knock came from the front of the house.

"Those television people won't let a body alone. Won't give up!" he snorted as he headed for the living room with a firm, pounding stride. Yanking the door open he confronted the knocker with, "I told you. . . ."

But it was not the red-coated female newsperson. This lady was gray-haired, rather pretty, wearing dark pants and a short dressy black-and-white-checked jacket. She appeared to be in her sixties, although Sol had never been much good at judging a woman's age. He stood there staring at her.

"You were expecting someone else, I take it," she said with a smile.

"I. . . . Yes. I mean, no," Sol stammered. "I just ran some nosy television newspeople off." He glanced past her. "You're one of 'em, are you?"

She shook her head. "I'm looking for Victor Timins. Does he live here?"

"No. He sure don't!" Sol's defenses jumped to attention again, figuring she wanted to see Vic about the mall. "You might as well forget it. I'm not gonna stand by and let my land be paved over. There'll be no stores on this place as long as I'm still breathin'."

She frowned. "I beg your pardon?"

"No need beggin' for nothin'. Won't' be no shopping mall here, and that's final!"

"Maybe we should make a fresh start. My name is Edgemont. Bea Edgemont. It was Braken for a few months, before my divorce." She waited, as though expecting the name to mean something. It didn't.

"I was married to Frank Braken for a while," Bea said. "His daughter is Victor Timins' wife."

It had not occurred to Sol until then, but he never had heard Frank's last name.

"You must be Victor's father."

Sol nodded his head up and then down once. "Too bad a father can't divorce a son."

She ignored the remark, inquiring instead, "Is Frank still with your son and his wife? I heard he came here after our divorce was finalized."

"Yep. He's still hangin' round. Vic lives over that way." Sol pointed off across the field. "In that new brick house off behind my barn. That's likely where you'll find Frank."

The woman started to turn away, then stopped. "It sounds as though you're not getting along too well with your son. I also sense you don't care much for my ex-husband."

"You could say that!" Sol admitted.

"What has Frank done to you and your family?"

The tone of Bea's voice aroused Sol's curiosity. He was warming to this woman. "I have a feelin' your Frank's put my son up to takin' my place away from me."

She shook her head. "He's not *my* Frank," Bea corrected. "I found that out soon after marrying him. It seems one woman in his life will never be enough for that man." Glancing away, she commented, "Wouldn't you just know he would still be up to no good?"

After a moment more she asked, "Do you have any knowledge of a gun collection Frank may have with him?"

"Sure do. They're up in my barn loft. In some wooden crates Frank's got stored there. Why?"

"Because they're mine. Frank took them out of storage when he left. I hadn't realized they were gone until a few days ago. That collection is priceless. My first husband, who passed away three years ago, spent a good part of his life as well as his income on that collection, buying here and there, piece by piece."

Sol was watching her closely. "You got proof they belong to you?" he asked. "I mean, if you can show me they're yours I'll sure let you have 'em. Every last one."

"I've brought some papers along." She opened her purse, taking out a couple legal-looking forms, handing them to Sol. "One is a copy of our divorce decree listing those things that were mine before I married Frank and were to remain in my possession. As you can see," she stepped around beside him to point out the paragraph, "the guns are listed right here as part of the property I was to retain. They're catalogued on the other sheet, along with each of their serial numbers."

After studying the documents, Sol handed them back. "Let's go to the barn to make sure they're the same guns? If they're yours, you can have 'em. Want nothin' to do with stolen property."

Bea placed a hand on Sol's arm. "Don't misunderstand. I'm not accusing you *or* your son of anything. I know Frank. I know how he operates. He most likely told you they were his."

"Didn't tell me nothin' until I happened to see what was in one of those crates. But you're right, he did make it sound like they were his."

"Tell you what, Mr. Timins—"

"Sol," he interrupted. "Call me Sol."

"All right, Sol. I'll go back to town, hire a truck and some men, then come back for the guns. I'm positive they're mine. But we'll check the serial numbers be-

114

fore taking them away. Would this afternoon be convenient for you?"

"Be just fine."

"Please don't say anything to Frank about my being here or that I'm coming after the guns." She smiled again. "I have a feeling I can trust you. Frank's hurt you too, hasn't he?"

"He's tryin'", Sol noted. "But I'm still on my feet. Not about to be counted out yet."

"Good for you!" she encouraged. "I don't consider myself down for the count either!"

They shook hands solemnly before Bea left. The phone was ringing as Sol closed the door. He hurried to answer it.

"You wanted to talk to me, Dad? I just got home. Nina told me you had called." Vic was shouting into the phone. "Can you hear me?"

"There'll be no shopping mall here. I'm puttin' a stop to it right now. Takin' you off that power of attorney you and Frank talked me into. May even write you out of my will, after I've given it a bit more thought. Now, what you got to say about that?"

"I'll be right over, Dad. We'll talk."

"No! We won't talk. Not today. You listen for a change." Sol took in a deep breath. He was feeling better as the frustration and hurt took wing on the heat of indignation. "Heard your big plans on the news last night for buildin' a shoppin' mall out here. The television people paid me a visit a while ago. I told 'em, as I'm tellin' you, there'll be no mall on my place as long as I'm alive. That's that. No need arguin' about it. No need even talkin' about it. That's just the way it's gonna be!"

"Dad, let me come over so we can talk. It's for you I'm—"

"No! You stay clear away from me. Don't want your face over here today. Or Frank's! Maybe tomorrow. Maybe I'll cool down some by then so we can talk." Remembering Bea was coming for the guns that afternoon, Sol added, "If I see you before tomorrow I'll have a lawyer out here so fast—I'll not only revoke that power of attorney, but my will as well, cuttin' you off at the knees. So for once in your life you'd better do as *I* say. Maybe tomorrow I'll feel like talkin'." With that, Sol slammed the phone back on its hook.

Hearing something, Sol glanced out to see a car roll to a stop by the house.

"Heard the news," Perry called as Sol went to see who was swooping down on him now. "What's going on, anyway? How come you're letting Vic build a mall on your land?"

"I'm not!"

Sol and Perry wandered out to stand by the fence looking off across the field where the mall was proposed to be built. Sol told Perry about the television news crew, his conversation with Vic, and Bea Edgemont's visit.

"Seems to me," Perry remarked, "Frank's been prodding Vic along on this. I have a feeling Teddy may have been right about Frank. Especially after what that Edgemont woman told you. I think Frank may have set you up to sign that power of attorney."

"Looks that way, don't it?" Sol agreed. "What hurts most is I don't know how much Vic's had to do with it. I'd like to think it was all Frank's doin's, but. . . ."

Sol sighed, then he turned to Perry as an idea took form. "How about helpin' me this afternoon?"

"With what?"

"Stick around until that woman comes back to pick

up her guns. Then drive over to Vic's place. Keep him and Frank busy talkin' while she gets the guns out of here. You might tell Vic you're worried about me. You know, after hearin' the news about the shopping mall. Act like you're beginnin' to agree with Vic's plans. Tell him you'll stop by to talk to me. That way we can keep him and Frank away till the guns are off my place."

Perry's eyes brightened. "I'll do it! Would be no lie. I *was* worried after hearing the news last night." Perry smiled, slapping Sol on the shoulder. "I haven't been involved in this much excitement since you and I ran off those hot-shot city hunters who thought their hunting licenses gave them the right to tramp over our land without permission."

"I recall that," Sol noted. "They threatened to shoot one of your heifers. But we didn't back down. No, sir! And I'm not about to now."

After making them each a sandwich at noon, Sol went with Perry to the barn to wait for Bea. Sol took some tools along to break open the crates when Bea arrived.

It was after two and Sol was growing nervous when a small van turned into the driveway, and pulled to a stop by the barn. The Edgemont woman followed in a large, expensive car. She got out as a soft rain began to fall and walked to the barn where Sol and Perry waited. Sol was thankful that the barn blocked a view of the van from Vic's place.

"I've hired these two men from a moving-and-storage company in Portland. I'll have them take the collection back for storage until I work out any legal problems Frank may raise. At least the guns will be safe so Frank can't sell them or try to make off with them again."

Sol grinned. "I'd have him arrested, if it was me." He knew he shouldn't enjoy the thought of Frank landing in jail. But he did.

He told Bea his plans to send Perry to his son's place to keep Vic and Frank occupied. But then a thought struck him. "What if they aren't there? What if they stop by while we're loadin' the guns?"

Perry was nodding. "I've been thinking about that. Why don't I go in and call Vic? If he's there I'll tell him I want to come by to talk to him. That way we'll know if he's home and keep him there."

"Good idea." Sol smiled again.

Bea and the two men waited while Sol and Perry went to the house. They were back within minutes. "Vic's home," Sol called as he neared the barn. "I figure Frank's there with him."

Perry was already in his car, waving as he pulled out, heading down the driveway faster than Sol ever remembered seeing him drive. Sol motioned the woman and the two men to follow him. Bea climbed the ladder easily behind Sol. Going directly to the damaged crate, Sol placed the point of his crowbar under a board, popping it off. With the men's help the guns soon lay in a row on the loft floor. Reaching for a flashlight Sol searched out the serial numbers, holding the beam steady as Bea and one of the men checked them off the list.

It did not take long. Every gun in the crate matched the recorded numbers. With half still unaccounted for, Sol went to another crate, ripped into it without a thought, to find only odds and ends of personal items. He went on to a third. There they found the rest of the guns. Soon the collection was packed away in special boxes the movers had brought with them, then the guns were loaded into the van.

Bea shook Sol's hand. "Thank you, Sol. You're a very special gentleman. Don't let Frank get the best of you, now." She pulled back, fishing around in her purse. "I want you to have my phone number in case you need to reach me. Also, here's my lawyer's card. Frank's going to blow up when he learns what we've done. He can call my lawyer if he has anything to say. I've moved from where I lived before, and my phone's unlisted. I don't want Frank to get hold of it."

"He won't get it from me!" Sol assured her. "Now you take care and don't get involved with any more of Frank's kind."

She shook her head. "You can be sure, I won't. Once burned is once too much for me."

Sol felt good as he watched her drive away, following the van down the driveway.

A short time later Perry returned. He was chuckling as he got out of his car. "I think I did a pretty fair job, if I do say so myself. I see what you mean about Frank. There's a mean temper brewing under the surface there."

"Maybe he suspected something. Most times he's as smooth as mustard on a hot bun when Vic's around." The two stood leaning against Perry's car in the lightly falling rain. "Did Vic mention the mall, or the power of attorney?"

"Never said a thing about the power of attorney. I didn't give him a chance to bring up the mall. I came right out and told him you wouldn't stand for it. He said he was doing it for you. Said he intends using your savings besides borrowing on his own place."

"He said that?"

Perry nodded. "I told him you'd never stand still for a mall being built here. He had no comment, just went right on telling how he was going to put your house up for sale as soon as he got you settled in that retirement complex south of town. Claims you haven't been yourself since he came back to Oregon."

As Perry talked on, Sol's mind could not get past Perry's comment about the savings account. "You say Vic planned to get into my savings?"

"That's what he said."

"Without my say-so?"

"Don't need it as long as he's got that power of attorney, Sol. That thing's hanging over you like an ax by a thread."

"Well, you can bet he's not gonna keep it hangin' there! I'll tell you, him, and the whole world he's not!"

As soon as Perry left, Sol went to the house and called Vic again, ordering him to come right over. "I've changed my mind about seein' you today. You'd better bring Frank along, too," Sol said before hanging up, without giving Vic a chance to reply.

10

Breaking Loose

Tense as a new father awaiting the birth of his first-born, Sol paced from living room to kitchen and back again, glancing out one window and then another as he watched for Vic and Frank. Detouring by way of the bathroom, Sol stopped in front of the mirror to gaze at his reflection.

"No fool like an old fool, they say," he muttered to the man staring back at him. He closed his eyes. "My Friend, I need you to get me through this. Don't want to be sayin' or doin' somethin' wrong again. And, knowin' me, I'm liable to do just that."

He was still standing there when he heard footsteps coming through the kitchen. Sol drew in a deep breath and squared his shoulders, reaching the living room as Vic entered with Frank.

"Oh, there you are, Dad. Perry told you our plans, I suppose. He said he was coming here after leaving my place."

"He did. Told me what you said. All you said! Heard it first on the news last night."

"I'm sorry about that. I wanted to keep it from you until I had everything worked out. I didn't know they'd flashed it over the tube until later when my phone started ringing itself hoarse. Didn't stop until late last night."

Vic continued, "It's going to take awhile to get everything in place so we can start building. You're not going to have to lift a hand, though. I don't want you worrying about a thing."

"Like the blue blazes!" Sol exploded, the smoldering anger spewing from him. At once he regretted his outburst, but on second thought decided he really didn't care. "Sit down! Both of you."

Taken off guard by his father's assertiveness, Vic stood rooted to the spot.

Sol pointed to the couch. "Sit, I said!"

Vic sat, motioning to Frank.

"Just you wait a minute! I'm not about to be ordered—" Frank began.

Vic cut him off through clenched teeth, patting the space beside him. "Sit down, Frank."

The man sat, choosing a wooden rocker instead.

Remaining on his feet, Sol glared down at the younger men, then turned to his son. "I not only know about your plans, Vic, but I'm tellin' you here and now this is where they stop. I realize I'll have no say what happens to my place after I'm gone. But I haven't checked out yet and don't plan to for some time."

"I'm doing this for you," Vic insisted. "I explained that to Perry."

"Perry was just playin' you for a fool. It was me sent him over to your place to keep you and Frank out of what hair I have left while I took care of somethin' here."

Sol turned to Frank. "As for you. . . . Guess it's time you were told your guns, or I should say Bea Edgemont's guns, were moved out this afternoon. I learned how you'd snatched 'em away from your ex-wife."

Frank grabbed the arms of the rocker as though to lunge to his feet, but Sol had moved up closer standing directly over him. "You. . . ." Frank sputtered. "You let that woman get away with my guns? Why, I'll nail both your hides out to dry. I'll have you arrested!"

"Weren't your guns to begin with, Frank. You know that." Sol was surprised by his own calm. His voice was well under control. "She's got legal papers provin' they're hers. I checked the serial numbers against the numbers on a list stating the guns were to remain her property after your divorce. They never were yours. Never will be yours. Not after today."

"Bea?" Vic inquired of Frank. "Your ex-wife? What's going on?"

Frank ignored the question.

"That's right," Sol said, stepping back away from the man."She came by this mornin'. Told how he," Sol gestured toward Frank with a thumb, "made off with her late husband's guns after she and Frank divorced. She was lookin' for you. Heard Frank was with you and his daughter."

A thoughtful frown creased Vic's forehead. "Frank? What's all this about?"

"None of your business." His words ground out like gravel through a crusher. "It doesn't concern you. Neither of you."

Vic stood to his feet as Frank shot out of the rocker to tower over Sol. Moving between the two, Vic faced Frank. "You told me those guns were part of your divorce settlement. That your ex-wife wanted nothing to do with them."

"She owed me. I had something coming for what I went through, married to that woman."

"You mean you just took them? I recall when you

first met her you told me her former husband owned a gun collection. You said then they were worth a fortune to the right people."

Retaining his clenched-fist stance, Frank stared past Vic at Sol. "That old man had no right letting her take them. They were mine. In my possession. You're losing as well as me, Vic. You're losing the money from the sale of those guns I was going to invest in your mall."

Sol was straining now to get around Vic. "You were what? What's that you say?" Vic put an arm up to hold his father back. "You mean you were goin' into partnership with Vic on that mall? The both of you were just gonna help yourselves to my land, as well as my bank account, like you helped yourself to Bea's gun collection?"

"It's to be a three way split," Frank said, seeming to realize he had said too much.

"It's gonna be nothin'!" Sol declared.

"Why, you meddling old fool. . . . I have plans for my share of the profits," Frank blustered. "Besides, with that power of attorney Vic has, you have no more say."

"Now hold on, Frank," Vic broke in. "That's enough! I'm not going to let you talk to my father that way."

A calm stole over Sol as he stepped around Vic to stand beside his son, the two facing Frank down together. "It was *you* who came in the middle of the night a few days back, wasn't it? You who tried to make me think I was losin' my senses."

"I had nothing to do with those things you found in your kitchen. . . ." Frank stopped again, flustered.

But Sol was smiling. "Interestin' you should know I found somethin' in my kitchen, seein' as how I've never mentioned it to anyone but Perry and young Teddy."

Frank shrugged. "I must have heard it from Perry."

"No, you didn't. He wouldn't have told you a thing. It was him and Teddy who first figured it might be you who did it."

Frank made a move toward Sol, a murderous anger flushing his fat face.

But Vic stepped in the way again. "That's enough, Frank. Go back to my place. We'll talk when I get home." He pulled his keys from a pocket. "Here, take my car. I'll walk back through the field."

Fury smoldered in Frank's deep-set eyes as he headed for the kitchen and then on out the back door.

Vic heaved a heavy sigh. "There's a lot here I don't understand, Dad."

Wearily, Sol sank to his chair, his first burst of anger having spent itself. He was exhausted. Vic sat back on the couch, leaning forward, thoughtfully rubbing his palms together as they listened in silence to Vic's car roar out the driveway.

At last Vic spoke. "You've been playing me for a fool ever since I came back to Oregon. I caught on to it awhile back. At first I figured it was the shock of losing Mom. Now I don't know what to think."

"I wasn't doin' so good when you came back. I needed you, but not as a nursemaid. *Or* as a parent. I needed your support. But you had no right takin' over things."

"I didn't—"

"You did! What about sellin' my cattle?" Sol demanded.

"That was for your own good, Dad."

Sol flayed the air with a hand. "Nothin' of the sort. It was pure orneriness. I've known a lot more about what's been goin' on than you've given me credit for. You thought I couldn't hear. Thought I couldn't think straight anymore. But I hear just fine, and I'm thinkin' better all the time." Sol stopped, his anger cooling. "Since I've been less than truthful with you, guess maybe a lot of what's happened has been my fault."

"I'd say so," Vic noted. "You've been lying to me."

Anger toned Vic's words, opening old wounds. Sol, his own anger nearly spent, listened as Vic related how he felt as a child growing up with a father who continually held his children at bay, never allowing them to draw close. Vic admitted it was probably guilt, more than anything, that had brought him back to the farm—guilt that the strain in their relationship had been partly his fault.

He turned then to the subject of the mall, outlining plans he and Frank had set in motion. "I did it for you, Dad. For all of us. It appeared you'd soon be unable to live by yourself. I knew it wouldn't work for you to move in with us. You've made it plain how you feel about Nina. I saw this as the only way left. Money from the sale of the mall would make it possible for you to live well for the rest of your life in a place where you'd be taken care of."

"What was it *you* intended gettin' out of it? Frank, it seems, planned on stackin' up a pile for himself."

Vic shook his head as though to clear it. "I needed all the capital I could lay my hands on to qualify for a loan. That was the only reason I was letting Frank in. He offered to invest what he had, as well as what he intended to get from the sale of those guns. I had no intention of holding anything out for myself. All the profit, except for Frank's share and paying myself back, would have gone directly into an account for you. That's the solid truth, Dad, whether you believe it or not. Actually, at this point it makes little difference what you believe."

His son's words and tone left a raw cut. Sol took note of the hurt reflected in his son's revelations. "From what Perry said, you were gonna dip into my savings, too. Just help yourself. Is that right?"

Vic reluctantly nodded, refusing to look at his father. "I was going to use my own as well, besides borrowing on my house. After the mall was built and the stores leased, we'd have sold it, paying off the loans and restoring our bank accounts before splitting the profits, with my share going to you. Frank was to get only a small share."

Sol was shaking his head. "I can't believe you'd just take what's mine like that. You'd do that to your own father?"

"You haven't been listening, Dad. I was under the impression you were incapable of thinking clearly or living alone. It was you who made me believe that. And, as for being my father, you were never much of a father to either Janet or me," Vic accused.

"I'm afraid you're right about that," Sol agreed, stung by the truth of his son's words. "I did pull back from the two of you. It was wrong. I know that now. You've no idea what a hollow feelin' I've carried all those years, standin' outside the circle of my own family just lookin' in.

"Had no memory of how a father was supposed to act, never havin' been close to my own. At least I wasn't hard on you, the way your grandfather was with me. Used to hurt some, seeing how gentle he could be with you when you were a tad. Didn't understand why he couldn't have been like that with me, his own son. Maybe he didn't have much fatherin' himself. Maybe he just didn't know how. Like me."

He smiled, although pain lay open in his eyes. "Suppose it's too late for us, Vic? Too late for a father and son after all these years?"

Vic stared at his father until a smile slowly eased across his face. "I think I like you better already. You're a crafty old coot. But you've got to stop playing games."

Sol nodded. "Games are over."

They sat talking, remembering and regretting the past right up to the present. Sol told Vic about finding the house disturbed a few nights back, and his suspicions of Frank.

"So," Vic breathed, "that's why there was mud on our floor the other morning. Frank knew I kept your house key on a peg by the door. It *must* have been him." He looked closer at his father. "You didn't really think I'd do that to you, did you?"

"Wasn't sure," Sol admitted. "At first I thought I'd gone completely off my rocker. That's why I went along with that power of attorney. Then I began smellin' the stink of a rat, my nose takin' me straight to either you or Frank."

An hour passed. At last Vic returned home, borrowing his father's barn boots for the walk across the field. Half an hour later Sol's phone was ringing.

"Frank's gone," Vic spoke in a hushed voice. "Packed a bag and called a taxi. He told Nina we'd had words. Said he'd be back later for the rest of his things."

Sol was relieved, but wondered about Nina. "How's your wife takin' it?"

"I'm not sure. She's in the spare bedroom right now straightening up the mess Frank left when he packed out of here in such a hurry. Evidently he didn't tell her what happened. I haven't either."

"I think you'd better. She needs to know," Sol noted.

Early the next morning Vic stopped by with the power of attorney in hand. "I brought this over so you could tear it up. I'm on my way to town to withdraw my request for a zone change."

Taking the paper, Sol smiled. "It don't seem like such a threat now. Think I'll put it in my safe-deposit box in case a day comes when I *do* need your help."

They sat and talked again, remembering happier times when Vic was growing up on the farm. Sol was warming to their new openness. And yet he was wary, too.

That weekend he helped Ted ready the team and wagon for use. Nina kept wedging into Sol's mind as he sanded and painted the old metal wagon tongue. He'd never allowed himself to get to know Nina, never welcomed the dark-haired young woman to the family. He'd remained cold, making excuses so he wouldn't have to be around her. Maybe she *didn't* have anything to do with Vic's divorce. It certainly was not her fault she'd been saddled with Frank for a father. Vic seemed to be in love with her, and the times Sol saw them together Nina appeared to appeciate Vic.

Finally one night, after trying to dislodge Nina from his mind all day, Sol forced himself to face what he had done to her as well as to his son and daughter. Sitting on the edge of the bed before turning in, Sol reached out to his ageless Companion.

"My Friend, seems I've got some straightening out to do with you as well as them. Appears you're not about to give me any peace till I do." Sol sat quietly for a time, praying and thinking. Other things came to mind, weighing heavily on his consciousness. He had to stop lying. All those times he'd colored the truth to suit himself had been nothing but out-and-out lies.

"Unchristian—that's what it's been. Thought I was bein' crafty, but it was only lies, Lord. Can you—*will* you forgive me?"

There in the dimly lighted bedroom the realities of what he had done over the past few months bombarded him. "Sin. That's what it was." Slipping painfully from the bed to his knees, he buried his face childlike on doubled fists.

"Lord—forgive me. Forgive and help me. Show me how to undo what I've done to Nina and Vic. Help me stop the lies. I've looked to you as a Friend for so long I plumb forgot who you really are—Lord of the universe, Creator, Savior. Forgive and help me clear up this mess I've stirred up for us all."

The following morning Sol felt more peace than he had known in months. In his inner being he knew God had heard and forgiven him. It was then that he realized Christmas was nearly upon him. A good time, he decided, to reach out to Vic and Nina. With that decision made, after taking care of the horses, Sol walked off across the wet, spongy field to Vic's new house for the first time since his son and Nina had moved in. Jake trailed behind, lying down with a grunt by the back door to wait under the roof overhang.

Nina came in answer to Sol's knock. "Why, Father Timins!" Her voice reflected her surprise at seeing him there.

Sol nodded a greeting. "Thought I'd take a walk and ended up over here." His habitual stretching of the truth to fit his own purpose chewed at him. Lord, I've got to stop this, he silently sent an S.O.S. winging. "Is Vic home?"

The dark-haired woman shook her head. Her collar-length black hair curled about her oval face, framing the olive tone of her skin. She was a good-looking woman, he had to admit. His resentment of her had never been fueled by anything she had said or done. He'd just had a hard time accepting Vic's divorce and remarriage.

Nina was holding the door open, motioning him in. "Vic's gone to town. He should be home before long."

Sol entered the kitchen. It was as clean as Ruth's used to be, but without those fragrant cooking smells he remembered when he came in from the barn or field. Sol glanced around. The bright countertops held a number of small electrical appliances beneath richly polished dark-wood cabinets. Cheery Christmas decorations warmed the room with color. Ruth would have loved a kitchen like her son had provided for his wife. A stab of regret nudged Sol. Had he neglected Ruth's needs?

He accepted a cup of coffee at the counter as Nina sat beside him on a high padded bar stool. Gazing into his cup, Sol asked, as though it had just occurred to him, "Heard anything from your father?"

"Just a postcard. I expect him back one of these days to pick up his things. Evidently he and Vic had words. Dad never said what happened and Vic refuses to talk about it."

Changing the subject, she looked closely at him. "Vic tells me you're feeling better."

"I'm keepin' busy. Let myself go there for a while after Ruth passed on. But I'm beginnin' to come out of it. I like havin' the horses around. Ted and his boy come over every day to take care of 'em. I been helpin' some, too."

"Vic worries about you." Her voice held genuine concern.

"No call to. Takin' better care of myself now than I was."

A car could be heard outside.

"That must be Vic," Nina commented, going to the window. "No! It's Dad!" she excused herself, running out to greet Frank.

Sol stepped to the window, watching with resignation as Frank eased his bulk from the taxicab. Going back to the counter, Sol waited until Nina came back into the house with her father.

The man stopped short when he saw Sol. "What are *you* doing here?"

"Why, Dad. . . ." Nina turned to him. "Sol's just visiting. This is the first time he's been to the house since we moved in."

The man appeared uncertain as to what to say. Looking from Sol to his daughter he asked, "Have you been told why I left?"

With Nina's back to him, Sol signaled Frank with a shake of his head.

"No," she was saying. "I understand you and Vic had some kind of disagreement. It's not the first time."

"But it is the *last!*" Frank declared. "I've come after the rest of my things. I'll be leaving then for good." He looked again at Sol. "I'll be over to your place later with a truck to load what's left of my crates."

"Fine," Sol said with a nod, his tone chilling.

"Oh, come on, Dad. You and Vic will work this out. You always have before. After all, it's Christmastime. Stay with us. At least through the holidays."

"After what Vic and this old man did to me? They've destroyed everything. You have no idea what this family you've married into is really like. No idea at all."

A softening settled over Frank as he pulled Nina to him, his hands on her shoulders. "Honey, I think you'd better come with me. I can't stand the thought of leaving you here with them."

"You want me to leave Vic?" Nina stepped back to look at her father. "What on earth has happened?" She turned to Sol. "Someone had better tell me. And right now!"

Sol slipped from the stool. "You wait just a minute, Frank. Don't go tryin' to break Nina and Vic up. You've made mess enough of your own life."

Her hands on her hips, the young woman stepped back so she could see both men. "All right! It's time someone told me what happened."

"This old man," Frank began, "took what was mine and gave it away. Things I had stored in his barn—that gun collection I got as a settlement when Bea divorced me. Then, after I yelled about what he'd done, Vic sided with him. That's when I realized they intended to rip me off."

"Those guns were never yours," Sol declared in a faltering voice, taking a hesitant step toward Frank. "They belong to Bea, and you know it!"

"They *used* to belong to Bea. She let me have them when we separated. They were payment for what I'd put into the house we bought together. After all, I turned the whole thing over to her when I left." Frank looked at Nina. "Then Bea comes along with some trumped-up paper saying I stole the guns from her. So what does Sol do? He lets her take them. Every last one. Now she's got the house *and* the guns, and I've got nothing."

"That's not the way it was," Sol said, making an effort to explain.

"Didn't Bea show you what appeared to be a legal paper?" Frank questioned. "And didn't you let her take the guns?"

"Well, yes, but—"

"That collection is worth plenty to the right people," Frank continued, ignoring Sol. "I put all I'd saved into that house Bea and I bought when we got married. Now I've lost it."

"Nina. . . ." Sol began. But a brittle chill was glazing the young woman's eyes. Sol stopped. What more could he say? Factwise, Frank was right. The way he'd said it, though, made it appear wrong *had* been done to him. "That's just not the way it was," Sol insisted.

"It's not?" Frank's voice was sarcastic. "The money I put in the house is gone. The guns are gone."

Sol sighed. "Frank, you stole those guns."

"It would be best, I believe, if you left now," Nina spoke quietly to Sol, handing him his jacket and cap. "There's no sense going over this all again and again."

Taking his things from her, Sol turned his back to Frank. "Listen to Vic's side of it when he comes home, Nina. At least do that much."

It was a miserable old man who walked home across the field with his dog trailing at his heels. "You know, Jake, I warned Vic he should tell her what was goin' on. Appears now like I *did* pull a shady deal on Frank."

Jake ignored him.

Glancing heavenward, Sol heaved a sigh. "My Friend, I've been none too smart through all this. If I'd talked to Vic about my feelin's a long time ago, maybe things wouldn't have gone this far."

The next morning, Saturday, the phone was ringing before Sol was fully awake. He hurried out to answer it and found Vic on the line. "I heard you were here yesterday when Frank came back."

"I was."

"Thought I'd let you know he's gone."

"Good!" Sol noted with satisfaction. Now maybe they could settle down in peace.

"No, Dad, it's not good. He took Nina with him."

11

A Search for Answers

"He what?"

Sol couldn't believe it. Why would Nina just up and leave? Hadn't she been able to see through Frank yet? But then, he *was* her father. And he was a talker. Sol's confrontation with the man in Nina's kitchen the previous morning flashed back into his mind. He had been unsuccessful in unraveling the tangles of Frank's twisted reasoning.

"Talking Nina into leaving was probably his way of getting even with me," Vic said.

"Didn't you tell her what happened? About the guns Frank had hidden away in my barn?"

"I didn't get a chance. She was in the bedroom packing when I got home. She seemed confused. I could see she'd been crying. Said she wouldn't talk about it right then and was going away for a while to think things through."

Sol's mouth dried to dust as a cold dread stabbed him. This was his fault again. His playacting and the lies he'd told had set the stage for what was happening to them. Not only had he not been a good father, but he'd failed as a father-in-law. He was nothing but a foolish old man poisoning his family with one deceit after another.

"You don't think she's left for good, do you?" he asked finally, afraid of the answer.

"I don't know. She said she'd be spending Christmas with her aunt, Frank's sister, in Denver. That's where Frank went after leaving last time. As long as Frank's around, it's hard telling what Nina is liable to do."

Sol felt sick to his soul as he hung the receiver up. His lies. Frank's lies. They had caught Vic and Nina in the cross fire. He found himself praying as he went about his work that morning, unable to rid his mind of the hurt and trouble he'd raised. He visualized the Timins' family tree buffeted by his deceptions, its branches twisting and snarling with every lie. Even watching Ted ground-drive Mike and Bell that day did not dispel the aching throb.

The next morning, Sunday, Sol was up, shaved, and dressed in his old brown suit before breakfast. "Haven't worn these clothes since I followed Ruth's casket to the cemetery," he said to his mirrored image as he combed his fringe of hair. "It's about time I went to church, my Friend. About time I cleaned up my act. Time I quit lying, once and for all, and made things right."

But how? He had no idea where to start or what to do. The night before he had decided church might be the place to begin. He thought of calling Vic to see if he wanted to go along, but decided against it. Another time he'd ask Vic. He was not the best example of a Christian right now.

When he pulled into the church parking lot, he found people heading for the new building. He glanced at the old church they were tearing down, where so many memories lingered.

The large, new auditorium smelled of fir and pine from fresh-cut boughs that decorated the sanctuary with Christmas greenery topped by floppy red bows.

Sol noticed several people he knew, although most were strangers. Pastor Brock stopped to shake Sol's hand as he was hurrying down the aisle toward the front. Sol found a place for himself at the end of a pew close to the back. During the announcements and singing his mind continued its playback of the past few days. Even in church he could not rid himself of the pain plummeting his soul. He had hoped for, had prayed for, the Lord to somehow speak to him there. Maybe through the minister's message. And yet his concentration returned again and again to the hurts that bound him.

Pastor Brock was nearing the end of his sermon when Sol noticed the cloth covered trays by the altar. Communion! They were going to serve communion. He couldn't take part. Not now. Not after the things he'd done. What was he going to do? To sit there and *not* take the bread and juice as it was passed would be humiliating. He glanced around. Maybe he would slip out as soon as the sermon ended.

But when the message reached its conclusion and the last song had been sung, Sol was still rooted to the pew. Silver trays of broken bread and tiny, tinkling glasses of grape juice were being carried toward the back. Toward him. He reached for the tray as it was handed to him, hesitated, then passed it on without taking the bread symbolizing his Lord's body sacrificed for his sin. For his lies. . . .

He could not take part in such a sacred observance after all he'd done. Not yet. He hadn't been living his life as a Christian. He was ashamed. Had God really forgiven him? It was at that moment Sol knew he had to do something to try to make things right with those he'd hurt. With the Lord himself. Making excuses was not enough. But how? How could he do it?

The Lord, he decided, would have to come through, show him the way.

Sol passed the juice on without taking any. Another time, he told himself. It didn't matter what the others thought. God, his Friend, knew his heart and knew why he could not join in the communion feast.

Later, after a hurried sandwich at home, Sol walked across the field to Vic's place. His son was sitting in the sprawling, silent house alone.

"Heard anything from Nina?" Sol inquired, lowering himself onto the couch beside his son.

"No, and I can't even call her. I don't have her aunt's name or address. Didn't have brains enough to ask for it before she left."

After several minutes of trying to make conversation, Sol headed back home. What could he do to right the wrongs he had brought on them? He had already admitted to Vic he had not been telling the whole truth when he allowed Vic to think he was failing faster than he was. He'd asked Vic's forgiveness. He'd asked God's forgiveness. What more was there?

"Lord, You've got to help me. Show me the way. . . ."

Ted and his family were gone for the day. It was turning into a dull, dismal Sunday afternoon, with no rain or sun or even a hint of a breeze under low clouds glooming the land, darkening Sol's soul to deeper despair.

When finally he could stand it no longer, he went to the phone and dialed Pastor Brock's number. "Could I talk to you this afternoon?" Sol asked. "I've got to set some things right and I don't know how to go about it or where to begin. Would it be all right if I came over for a few minutes?"

The pastor agreed to see Sol and offered to drive over to his place. He arrived less than an hour later.

Sol met him at the front door. But when the minister left later, Sol found himself regretting his compulsion to talk to the man.

Sol had admitted his lies, telling what had recently occurred within his family, as well as relating what had happened with Frank and the guns he'd helped Bea recover. The minister prayed for him, which brought some relief to his bruised soul. But as the man was leaving he looked Sol straight in the eye and asked, "So, Sol, just how do you plan to right these wrongs you've been party to?"

But wasn't that why he had asked to talk to him? Sol already knew the questions. It was answers he needed. "Don't see how I can do anything," Sol noted, "what with Nina gone."

"Seems to me," Pastor Brock commented thoughtfully, "you need to talk to your daughter-in-law. Explain things as best you can."

Although Sol agreed, he had no idea how to go about it. Vic didn't even know how to get in touch with her. It appeared hopeless.

After supper, consisting of a bowl of cold cereal, Sol felt a compulsion to walk across the field to Vic's place again. He wasn't sure why. He opened the back door and called to his son. Getting no answer, Sol went on in to the front of the house. Vic was standing in the living room visibly shaken, staring down into the white marble fireplace, where an anemic flame struggled to subdue a thick oak log.

"I tried calling Nina, but she wouldn't come to the phone."

"Thought you didn't have her number."

"I remembered a letter she'd received from her aunt about a month ago. Found it under her jewelry box in the bedroom. I called information for the aunt's telephone number, for all the good it did me."

"She wouldn't talk to you?"

Vic shook his head. "It's not a good sign, Dad. Not good at all. If she just wanted to get away for a while, you'd think she'd at least be willing to talk. I see Frank's hand in this."

"Don't doubt it a bit." Sol rubbed his chin thoughtfully. "Do you think I should give it a try? Maybe she'll talk to me."

Vic looked at his father sympathetically. "I know you blame yourself, Dad. But I'm just as much at fault. I had no right trying to run your life. If I hadn't taken over, you wouldn't have done what you did and things would be different now."

"Let's not get ourselves in a stew over which one's the most at fault. At least let me try to call Nina. Couldn't make things much worse than they are right now."

Vic handed his father the envelope he'd found with the aunt's address. Vic had penciled the phone number on it. Sol picked up a pen and notepad from an end table and copied the number. Then, as Vic bent to stir the fire in the hearth, Sol quickly added the aunt's address, noting the letter had been sent from Denver.

It was nearly dark when Sol got back home. Shrugging out of his jacket, he went straight to the telephone. After dialing the number, Sol waited, wondering what he would say if Nina did come to the phone.

The receiver was picked up on the fourth ring. "Hello?" It was a woman's voice, although not Nina's.

"I'd like to speak to Nina Timins." The words sounded strange. He had never put Timins with Nina's first name before.

"Who's calling, please?"

"A neighbor. From Oregon. . . ." Sol stopped himself. "Tell her her father-in-law would like to talk to her."

There was a long silence before the woman responded with, "Just a minute. I'll see if she'll talk to you."

A muffled discussion followed. Then a man came on the line. It was Frank, his voice in perfect control. "Nina and I have nothing to say to either you or to Vic. We'd appreciate it if you would leave us alone."

Nina was probably there in the room with him, Sol decided. He was about to reply when the receiver was quietly replaced at the other end. Sol looked at the phone still in his hand, questioning aloud, "Now what?"

He slept fitfully that night. The next morning he realized with a jolt that it was December twentieth already, only five days before Christmas. It didn't seem possible. The year before he had been a widower for only two months when Christmas caught him unaware. Except for a phone call from Janet and another from Vic, last year's Christmas had been a day just like all the rest. The only evidence of the season had been the colorful Christmas cards that had arrived in Sol's battered mailbox. He'd set them around the living room, as he had again this year. Since he had not sent any cards out, however, this year's batch was noticeably smaller.

After taking care of the horses—for he had resumed those morning duties once again—Sol cleaned up and drove to town. He stopped first at a card shop where he bought Christmas cards for his grandchildren, as well as for Janet and her husband. He then went to the bank to transfer money from savings to checking. The next stop was the post office. Stamps in hand he stood at an island counter writing checks to enclose with each card, dropping them in the mail slot. He hoped they would reach his family in time.

On his way home he stopped by the hardware store, picking out some tools and gadgets for Vic. He lucked out, for the young man who had waited on him before offered to gift-wrap his purchase. Sol would liked to have mailed a gift to Nina, but thought better of it. It would be like rubbing salt in the wound, he supposed.

Christmas Eve morning arrived with Sol longing for past Christmases when the family had all been together. Ruth had made the house look so bright and festive. Well, he determined, he would make sure this year was different from the last. With that decided, he went to the phone and called Vic.

"It's Christmas Eve," Sol announced when his son answered. "Looks like it's just you and me. Let's do somethin' to make it special. How about comin' over this evenin'? We could watch the Christmas specials on television together."

There came a subdued groan over the line. "Dad, I'm just not in the mood."

"Neither am I. But it's the observance of our Lord's birth. We can at least try puttin' our own miseries aside for a few hours."

"You may be right," Vic acknowledged finally, without enthusiasm. "I was thinking of driving to town for a while. . . ."

"Oh. Well, how about going out to eat tomorrow?" Sol persisted. "I know there's just the two of us, but we're still a family. I spent last Christmas alone for the first time in my life. I'd rather not do that again."

There was a noticeable catch to Vic's voice. "I-I'm sorry, Dad. Last year I wasn't aware of how lonely it must have been for you. This year, with Nina gone, I understand how you must have felt. So, sure, we can go out for Christmas dinner."

That evening Sol found some carrots in the refrigerator and chopped them up as a Christmas Eve treat for the horses. He remembered his mother doing that when his dad had horses on the place. He then cooked and seasoned Jake's hamburger for a change, carrying it and the carrots to the barn. After all, he reasoned, hadn't the first Christmas taken place in a stable?

Back in the house he dialed Vic's number for the second time that day, hoping his son might have changed his mind about going to town. Going to a bar, Sol well knew. They could drag the old Monopoly board out. He recalled that Vic and Janet used to play Monopoly when they were youngsters. But there was no answer at Vic's end of the line.

Not about to give up, Sol rummaged through the cupboard until he located a half pack of popcorn, popped up a batch for himself, then put on a fresh pot of coffee. Armed with a bowl of buttered popcorn, a steaming cup of his favorite brew, a chunk of cheese, and an apple Vic had brought in from the orchard before the first frost, Sol settled himself in the living room in front of the tube.

When he tired of the usual Christmas repeats, he turned the set off and went to the bedroom for his Bible. He found the familiar story in the book of Luke. He began reading aloud the story of the birth of Christ, his voice filling the empty house with God's revelation. It brought him closer to his Lord and Friend. He thrilled once again to the happenings of some two thousand years before.

He continued reading until he heard a car at the back of the house. He got up, went out to the porch, and flipped on the yard light. It was Vic, as he hoped it would be. But when his son came through the door, Sol took note of his watery eyes and flushed face.

"Been drinkin', I see," he said, leading the way to the living room.

Vic nodded. "Some."

"Want a cup of coffee?"

"No. What's that? Popcorn?"

"Help yourself."

Dipping a cupped hand in the bowl, Vic asked, "Nina didn't happen to call, did she?"

Sol shook his head.

"This would have been Nina's and my first Christmas together. We were just about to go out and buy a tree when she left. I couldn't stand being alone there tonight."

"You might have come over here," Sol told him, a ring of hurt to his voice. "I've been alone, too, you know."

Vic looked even sadder. "I'm sorry. I lost track of time. Dropped by the house just now to see if Nina might have come home, but. . . ."

Sol nudged Vic toward a chair. "Better sit down."

Vic obeyed, a dazed expression clouding his face. Sympathy slipped over Sol. Vic appeared to have aged twenty years in the last week.

"Come on," he spoke gently. "The bed's made upstairs in your old room. You'd better stay the night. Shouldn't be drivin' in your condition. There's other folks out there on the roads, you know."

Tears moistened Vic's eyes. "Dad, I . . ."

"I know. I know," Sol crooned, taking his boy's arm. "Come on to bed. Tomorrow things may look better. Maybe Nina will call. If she doesn't find you home, she'll likely try here. We're just not gonna give up."

Vic allowed his father to lead him up the narrow stairs to the seldom-used room on the second floor. Coming back down, Sol picked up his Bible, carrying it to his own bedroom. Before easing himself into bed, he slipped to his knees in a quiet time of misery masked as prayer.

Christmas morning dawned cold and frosty-wet with a raw soul-chilling wind. Sol stared at the still-silent telephone when he came into the kitchen, the cold floor boards creaking underneath the linoleum with each step. What was Nina doing this morning? he wondered. What was she feeling?

After a hurried trip to the barn Sol came back to cook breakfast. It was a good feeling knowing his son was upstairs. Vic slept late, finally coming down glum and seemingly resigned that he would not be hearing from his wife that day. Sol made him toast and a glass of orange juice from a can nearly forgotten in the freezer. He then brought out the gift he had purchased for Vic a few days before and opened a package he had received from Janet. Inside was a bright red plaid shirt.

"I'm sorry I didn't get anything for you, Dad."

"That's all right," Sol noted. "Just bein' with you this year is gift enough."

Vic appeared pleased with the tools. "This must be the first time you've ever purchased a Christmas gift for one of us kids. Mom was always the gift-buyer for the family."

Sol sighed. "Yep, she surely was."

Later that afternoon, when Vic was feeling more human, they drove to town for dinner at the best restaurant they could find open. On the way they stopped by Vic's place, but nothing had changed there.

At first Sol tried lifting Vic's spirits as they sat in the strangely quiet restaurant. But nothing he said helped. He longed to point out how Vic's drinking was only plunging him deeper into depression. But he didn't. At last he gave up trying to make conversation and sat looking around at the other diners.

An elderly woman sat alone near the window, bent over a heaping plate of turkey, intent only on the food before her. Another lone diner—a man in a crumpled business suit—was seated off in a corner. A salesman, Sol speculated, probably caught away from home. There were no children in the room. The other customers were couples, no doubt without nearby family members with whom to share the holiday.

He thought again of Ruth. Would he ever get over missing that woman? No, he decided, not after nearly fifty years of marriage. He had been thinking about Janet lately. And of his grandchildren. He had maintained no close communication with any of them. And now Nina, too, was gone.

They left the restaurant and drove around the countryside, both dreading the return to their empty houses. At last, with the ordeal of Christmas over, Vic headed back to the farm and dropped Sol off before driving on home. Sol stood in the yard and watched as Vic drove down the driveway. With a sigh he ambled up the steps and went inside.

Janet phoned later—her usual holiday duty call. She asked what was new, but he couldn't bring himself to fill her in on Vic and Nina's troubles. He made an effort to answer her other questions. He had always found talking to his daughter a difficult task. He wanted to tell her he cared for her, that he missed her. But the words wouldn't come.

The next day Vic came by to tell his father he was driving to the beach for a few days to try to sort things out. He figured since Nina had not been in touch with him by now, she probably had no intention of ever coming back.

As soon as Vic left, Sol backed his own car out of the garage and drove to Pastor Brock's house. But the minister was not home. Desperately needing someone to talk to, Sol drove on to town and pulled up in front of Perry and Vera's house. He had been there only twice since the Marshes moved away from the farm. Vic had brought him both times.

Vera opened the door to Sol's knock. "Mornin'," Sol greeted the short, plump woman who had been Ruth's best friend. "I guess I should have called before comin' by like this. But didn't know I'd end up here until after I was on the road."

"Why, Sol! You never need an invitation to our house, and you know it! We've missed you and. . . ." She stopped, seeming not to know what to say.

"You miss her too, don't you?" he comforted gently. "You two used to help each other with your cannin', sharin' recipes, and secrets on how to manage your husbands."

Tears came to her eyes, which she quickly brushed away. "I'm sorry, Sol. My missing her can't come close to what you must be going through. She was a fine woman, Ruth was." Stepping back, she held the door open wider. "Well, come on in. Perry's there in the other room."

Sol followed her to the small living room to find Perry in a chair hunched over the coffee table where newspapers were spread, working on a disabled toaster. An artificial Christmas tree decorated a corner of the room.

"Look who I found on the doorstep, Perry." She turned to Sol. "Sit down. Take off your jacket. How about a cup of coffee? I recall you always liked your coffee."

"Still do," Sol noted with a smile. "But think I'll

pass. Been drinkin' too much lately."

Perry pushed the toaster away. "So, you finally dragged yourself into town to see us. About time, I'd say."

Sol eased himself down in the offered chair. "Felt the need to talk. Stopped by to see Pastor Brock, but he wasn't home. Thought I'd come on in here for a while. Hope you don't mind." He glanced first at Vera and then back to Perry.

"Oh, course we don't mind," Vera assured him. "You're welcome here anytime. What's wrong, Sol?"

"I've got myself and my family in a jam it seems. And I just don't know what to do about it."

12

Into the Wild Blue

"I told Vera about keeping Frank and Vic off guard while you helped that woman make off with those guns stored in your barn," Perry commented. "Is that what's causing trouble for you now, Sol?"

"That's part of it."

"I wondered if you might be herding yourself into a corner. Frank didn't appear to be the kind to roll over and play dead."

Sol filled Perry and Vera in, ending with, "The worst part is Nina leavin'. I wish I could do somethin' about it, but don't know how or what."

"Looks hopeless all right," Perry agreed with a shake of his shaggy head.

"Why, it is not!" Vera declared, standing to confront the two men. "You'd better just get yourself busy, Solomon Timins, and see to it that that couple gets back together."

"Don't get in a fuss, my love. Sol's done all he can. Things will work themselves out in time."

"He certainly has not done all he can!" the woman replied impishly, hands on her hips. "He ought to ask that woman, Frank what's-his-name's former wife, to send copies of those papers she showed Sol. Go see Nina. Show them to her. Insist she look at them."

"He'd have to go clear back to Denver to see Nina."

"That's a long drive in the dead of winter," Sol ventured. "Mountain passes must be heaped with snow by now."

"Sol, just where have you been the last few decades? There's jets now that fly us places lickety-split. Would take only a couple hours to get to Denver, find the address, and see that girl."

"I've never flown in my life, Vera. Never wanted to, and don't care to now."

"About time you did, then. Ruth would expect you to and you know it. Vic is her son. There's nothing she wouldn't do, or didn't do, for you and those two youngsters of hers." Vera planted herself across from Sol, leaning closer, her voice intent. "This is *your* son and *your* daughter-in-law we're talking about, Solomon."

"I know, but. . . ."

"Buts don't get the job done!" she interrupted. "Tell you what." She turned to her husband, who sat watching with an amused half smile. "Perry can go along with you! He's flown. He'll give you moral support."

"Now, wait a minute there," Perry said, holding up a hand. "It's mighty cold this time of year in the Rockies." He sat studying Sol. "You know though, she may have something. It would show Nina you cared. Even if you aren't able to talk her into coming back, it would give her something to think about."

"And, Sol," Vera added, "it would make you feel a whole lot better, knowing you'd tried."

And so two days later, after calling Bea to explain the situation, Sol and Perry boarded a jet for Denver. Vic had called from the coast a couple times to see if his father had heard from Nina. He decided that he might as well stay on there a few more days. Bea sent copies of the papers Sol had requested by next day air service. The documents were tucked safely in the breast pocket of Sol's brown suit as he walked the long tunnel-like ramp onto the blunt-nosed jetliner at Portland International Airport that Wednesday morning. He was thankful Vic had not returned from the coast yet, figuring it would be best if he didn't know what his father was up to until it was over and done.

Perry carried a small leather shaving kit while Sol toted his razor, comb, and toothbrush in a brown paper bag. He hadn't figured on needing much. After all, they were only going to be gone overnight. He wanted to be back before Vic, if possible. He just wished Perry had mentioned what he planned to wear. His friend's thick gray quilted jacket and freshly pressed navy slacks left Sol feeling shabby and out of place in his old brown suit.

Sol's stomach gave a lurch as the big jet taxied away from the boarding terminal. He'd never harbored a desire to fly and that feeling had not changed. But here he was, about to be jettisoned up through Oregon's heavy rain-swollen clouds, across two mountain ranges, to a city he knew next to nothing about.

Perry appeared relaxed in the aisle seat beside him. Sol glanced at him. "Doesn't it bother you? Flying, I mean?"

"Scared me near to death the first time! But I wasn't about to let on to Vera. She thinks flying's the most exciting thing that ever happened to her." He was smiling. "What's the matter, Sol? Is it getting to you?"

"Like I've heard said," Sol replied with feigned resignation, "it's not the going up that gets you down.

Got no roadsides up there to pull off on for repairs. Probably should have let Vic know I was goin'. Just in case somethin' happens."

"Didn't you say you told your neighbor? The one with the horses?"

"Well, sort of. Told him I'd be gone a couple days. Told him I was with you. Didn't mention flyin' clear off across country and back."

"Relax, Sol. Nothing's going to happen." Perry patted the back of Sol's hand where it gripped the armrest between them. "We're not going to crash.

"By the way, I thought you said you weren't going to keep Vic in the dark any longer. So how come you didn't tell him where you were going and why? What's he going to think if he comes home and finds you gone?"

"I didn't decide to do this until after he left for the coast. Saw no reason to bring it up when he called last. Left a note on my kitchen table sayin' I was with you in case he gets back before we do. Besides, he's been spendin' more and more time in town lately. If he comes home before me I figure that's probably where he'll head."

"Still drinking pretty heavy, is he?"

"Afraid so. Worries me some."

The jet had reached the end of the runway and was turning for takeoff. Sol took up the slack on his seat belt as a pretty, blond flight attendant walked the aisle of the half-filled jet checking on her passengers. A "fasten seat belt" sign continued to blink overhead. Sol pulled in a long, deep breath, then quietly panicked as he watched the flight attendant belt herself into a seat in front of them.

The whine of the jet's engines surged to a roar as they started down the runway, slowly at first, then at a dizzying speed. A tremor shuddered the fuselage. Sol glanced out the small window. The winter landscape, shrouded in drizzle, was rushing by, cast in a blur of grays and blacks. He closed his eyes and leaned back against the headrest. Why had he agreed to Vera's order to fly to Denver? Would the Lord protect him after all he'd done? A vision projected itself on his mind's screen of the plane crashing in flames. The din of the jet's big engines hammered in his brain as other equally horrifying fantasies bombarded him.

He opened his eyes and turned toward the window again as they reached the end of the runway. The ground was falling away fast beneath them as the jet thrust its nose upward. For a few brief seconds Sol felt sheer elation.

Then, high above the wide waters of the Columbia River, the plane maneuvered into a steep bank. Inside his chest Sol's heart beat out a silent S.O.S. A sensation of falling washed him. An urge to grab onto something gripped him. If he didn't he would fall. . . .

His hand moved involuntarily toward the seat in front, then stopped. Perry was watching. What good would it do anyway? Both he and the plane were suspended in air. He prayed as the jet climbed higher, aiming toward the east. At last a sense of well-being bathed him with a soothing flush, submerging his fears. Sol pulled in a deep, relieved breath, letting it slowly drain from him.

"Thank you, my good Friend," he spoke under his breath.

"What'd you say?" Perry asked.

"Just mumblin' to myself." Sol turned to the window again. "Is that normal? The wings out there are vibratin' up and down somethin' awful."

"Made to, they tell me. Thought my heart would stop when I noticed it the first time Vera and I went up. Didn't seem to bother her one bit."

Made to vibrate or not, it was disquieting. To keep his mind off the wings' tremor, Sol pulled a magazine from the seat pocket in front, pretending interest in the cover picture. He was getting tired hearing about the fearless Vera and her love of flying.

Perry chuckled. *"Glamour Doll Magazine?* Intending to do a bit of serious reading, are you, Sol?"

With a sheepish grin Sol shoved the magazine back.

They were flying now through thick, fog-heavy clouds. Just as Sol was wondering how the pilot could tell where they were, the plane broke through to meet the brilliance of the sun, warming his fears, lifting his leaden heart. He allowed the tension to completely drain from him as they skimmed clouds resembling a harvested cornfield blanketed by a fresh fall of pinkish snow. They appeared solid enough to step out on. The sky above was a spotless blue—clean and pure, devoid of man's clutter. God's creation. What, after all, was there to fear? Even if they did crash God was, after all, still in control.

As the jet nosed down for a landing at Denver through clouds emitting light, drifting flakes of white, Sol experienced a second anxious thrill. The ground was fast coming up to meet them. He felt a jolt as wheels connected to pavement. He was grateful to be rolling on solid ground once more.

Relieved that he was not alone, Sol followed Perry outside the air terminal where taxis lined the curb. Perry headed for the first one with Sol hustling along behind clutching his paper bag. Once settled in the back seat, Perry gave their driver the name and address of the hotel where the travel agent—one Vera had contacted—had booked reservations for them.

The room was small and sparsely furnished, with two beds on the fourth floor of an older stone building. Sol was thankful they shared a room. Big cities were alien lands, as far as he was concerned.

He sat on the edge of one of the beds. "It's not gonna be easy talkin' to Nina."

"I'm sure it won't. But you'll feel a whole lot better for the trying."

"I suppose. . . ." With the Lord's help, and Perry's, Sol intended to give it his best effort. Would that be enough? he wondered.

"You hungry?" he asked at last.

Perry shook his head. "Not after that—whatever it was—they served on the plane. Are you?"

"No. Think I'd like to go see Nina right away."

"Sounds good to me." Perry pulled his jacket on again. "Glad I wore this. Looks like the snow might pile up some before it's through." He glanced at Sol. "You warm enough in that thin suit jacket?"

Sol shook his head. "Didn't stop to think about it. Should have known better. But then, I didn't have anything else good enough to wear."

"Want to go buy something warmer?"

Sol glanced at himself in the mirror above the dark-wood-toned hotel dressing table. "Doesn't fit too good anymore, what with all the weight I lost this past year. But, can't see buyin' somethin' for just one day's use. We'll be home tomorrow."

"All right. Let's go then."

They were walking down the carpeted hallway when Sol stopped short. "How do we go about findin' the address?"

"We give it to a cab driver and let him worry about it. I was thinking though, maybe you should call Nina first to make sure she's home."

"It's best if I don't. If I called she might leave."

"What do you intend to do about Frank?"

Sol shrugged as they stepped onto the elevator. "I have no idea. Will decide that when the time comes."

He had never ridden in a taxi before coming to Denver. The high-priced transportation did not set well. A bus would have been cheaper. But, he had to admit, it was a simple way of finding Nina without searching all over the place.

It stopped snowing by the time the taxi pulled up in front of a small, boxlike, white frame house on the outskirts of town. Bare tree limbs sparkled under a thin frosting of crusted snow in the yard, catching the sun's beam through a break in the clouds.

"Well, guess I'd better get this over with," Sol said as he pushed the car door open. A bracing chill from off the high Rocky Mountains hit him full in the face as he got out.

"I'll wait here," Perry told him. "You'd better try talking to her alone."

Sol nodded. "If I'm able to."

He was not looking forward to going into that house by himself. Snow crunched under his thin-soled brown oxfords as he carefully navigated the partially swept walk. Rock salt had been sprinkled around the door and porch platform. He pressed the icy bell button and a faint ringing resounded from somewhere inside. There followed the sound of foot-falls that grew louder. Sol sucked in a deep breath, hitched his shoulders back, and waited. He hoped Frank would not be the one to open the door.

A woman, round-faced and serious of eye, stood in the open doorway dressed in a shapeless gray woolen dress and, in what Ruth used to call, sensible black shoes.

"Afternoon," Sol spoke with a nod. "Would Nina happen to be home? Nina Timins?"

"She is." The woman appeared to be in her late fifties, but Sol had never felt competent in judging a woman's age.

A blast of wind sent a shiver through him. "Didn't dress warm enough for your winter. Doesn't usually get this cold back in Oregon."

"Oh. . . . So you're from there." She shoved the door partially closed, peering out through a foot-wide crack. It was plain his appearance on her doorstep brought no joy.

"Yes, ma'am. I'm Solomon Timins. Nina's father-in-law. I flew out this mornin' to talk to her. When I've done that I'll be headin' back."

She was glaring at him, her eyes scrutinizing the man before her with a bit more interest than at first. Sol could well imagine the stories she had heard about him and Vic and all that had gone on. He braced himself. He could not, would not, allow this woman to block him from seeing Nina. He took a firmer grip on his sagging determination.

"I don't believe Nina cares to talk to you, Mr. Timins." Her words came out clipped and brittle. "Perhaps it would be best if you caught an earlier flight out."

"No, ma'am." Sol shaded his words with a forcefulness he was not feeling. "I'll leave as soon as I've had a few minutes with my daughter-in-law. I've hurt her. I've come to apologize, to try to make things right. Soon as I've had my say I'll be leavin'."

Her gaze hardened, reminding Sol of Frank. He returned her stare without a blink. At last she sighed and stepped back, opening the door wider. "Oh, all right. You can come on in, I suppose. I'll tell Nina you're here and see if she wants to talk to you."

Gratefully Sol entered the warmth of the house, remaining in the living room while she went to find her niece. He glanced around the small room furnished with scarred and worn bits and pieces that didn't quite match. Certainly nothing like the home Vic had provided Nina.

At last the dark haired young woman appeared. "Father Timins! What on earth are you doing here?" she asked abruptly as she came into the room. She wore dark slacks and a heavy turquoise sweater. "Did Vic send you? Did he come, too?"

Sol shook his head. "Vic doesn't know I'm here." He glanced at Nina's aunt, who stood just behind her. "If you don't mind. . . . I realize this is your house, but I would like to talk to my daughter-in-law alone."

Nina nodded to the woman, who turned abruptly and left without a word. She motioned toward a chair and Sol stiffly sat down, his fingers aching from the cold as he reached for the document copies Bea had provided. He took them from his inside jacket pocket, glancing at Nina as she sat in a small, once plush chair across from him. She seemed so young. Defenseless. A nudge of pity enveloped him.

"I'm sorry about the trouble I've been party to between you and Vic. I never welcomed you proper when he brought you to Oregon as his wife. That was wrong. *I* was wrong.

"I intentionally gave Vic the impression I wasn't able to do for myself. Maybe. . . ." The whys of what he'd done became clear at that moment as he faced the young woman. He had been telling himself he was getting even with Vic, pretending still to be locked in the debilitating depression that had held him prisoner after Ruth's death. But that was not the whole of it. "I wanted Vic to feel sorry for me. I wanted what

I'd never been man enough to earn before—my son's attention."

"It's called love, Father Timins," Nina said. "But it's never real when earned through deception."

Sol shrugged. "I know." He shook his head. "I know too I'm responsible for you and Vic breakin' up."

Nina shifted uncomfortably in her chair. "You mean, because of what you did to my father?"

"No. That's one thing I don't regret. Although I did handle it wrong." He unfolded the papers he had been holding. "These are copies of Frank and Bea's divorce agreement. Bea sent them so I could prove to you those guns are hers. Shows, too, your father didn't put anything into that new house they bought after they got married. The money came from the sale of the house Bea owned before she married Frank. He had no call, that I can see, takin' those guns as repayment. None at all."

Nina reached for the papers, glancing at them. "But Dad said. . . ." She stopped. "May I keep these?"

Sol nodded. "Just don't let Frank see 'em. There's a lot of lawyer stuff you'll have to wade through. I understood most of it. I marked the places where the guns and house are mentioned."

Nina folded the papers, slipped them into a magazine from an end table beside her and clutched the magazine to her. "How is Vic? He's called, but I didn't feel like talking to him. I need more time to think things through."

"I called you, too."

"I know."

"Vic was real upset when you left. Never seen him so down. It's been hard knowin' a good part of it has been my doin'. If I'd been the sort of father I should have been, Frank couldn't have pulled our family apart the way he did."

Anger flushed her face. "It's unfair blaming everything on Dad. He's been hurt, too."

"Read those papers before you make a judgment on who's most to blame. Actually, I guess we've all done some wrong. Every single one of us."

A door banged at the back of the house as a man's voice penetrated the living room. "What's that taxi doing out front?"

Quickly Nina rose to her feet. Lowering her voice she whispered, "Dad's home. He was next door at a neighbor's. You'd better go. He's still pretty angry."

Sol stood up. "All right. I'll be on my way. But, Nina, please think about comin' back to Vic. Back to Oregon. I'd like to make it up to Vic *and* to you. I'd like us to be a real family."

"I had hoped for that when we first went to Oregon. I was so excited about building a house on the farm where Vic grew up. But right from the start you wanted nothing to do with me."

At that instant Frank burst into the room still wearing his heavy jacket and squared-off kinky brown fur cap pulled low over his narrow eye slits. He stood there, filling the living room with his brooding presence as his sister came to stand behind him. "You'd better leave, Sol. You're not welcome here in this house."

"I thought this was your sister's place," Sol replied with an unexpected calm. "Or do you consider everything you happen on as yours to do with as you see fit?"

Nina moved closer to her father. "Sol just came to apologize."

"Oh? He has, has he?" Frank's voice oozed with sarcasm as he questioned, "And did he happen to recover my gun collection? Or the money he lost for me when he let that woman make off with them?"

Staring at Sol, Frank demanded of him, "Is that why you came here, old man?"

13

Mending the Gap

Nina placed a restraining hand on her father's arm. "We were just talking."

Ignoring the man, Sol spoke to directly to Nina. "There's a taxi waitin' out front for me. I'm flyin' home in the mornin'." He started for the door with her following. Sol lowered his voice. "I'm stayin' at the Capital Hotel, room 406, should you want to talk."

She nodded. "Tell Vic. . . . Never mind. I'll be in touch with him later."

Sol heard the door close behind him as he carefully made his way along the icy walk to the curb where the taxi's motor was still running. Perry pushed the back door open and Sol slid in beside him.

"How long was I gone?"

"Fifteen, twenty minutes maybe. How did it go?"

The cab driver was watching them in the rearview mirror. "Where to?"

"Back to the hotel," Perry told him, turning again to Sol. "Did you see her?"

"I did. Frank wasn't there at first. He just walked in."

"I saw him. He came from the house next door. Seemed surprised when he saw the taxi."

"Oh? I thought his sister might have called to tell

him I was there. But maybe she didn't. Could be she's beginnin' to see through him. He's tryin' to keep Nina from the truth."

Once they got back to the hotel, Perry had a time talking Sol into leaving the room long enough to get something to eat. "Don't want to miss the call if Nina decides to get in touch with me," Sol told him. But at last he agreed to go for a quick meal in the hotel dining room. He returned to the room alone to wait beside the silent telephone. Switching the television on for company, he stretched out on the bed while Perry went for a walk.

When Perry returned he noted it was snowing again. Sol wondered aloud if they would be able to return home in the morning if the weather worsened. But by daylight the snow had stopped with only a couple inches more on the ground.

Since breakfast was to be served on the plane, they hurried down to flag another taxi to take them to the airport. Sol had heard nothing from Nina. Nothing at all. Had he made a needless trip? he wondered. Had he nearly frozen himself to death in Colorado's high country for nothing?

Their flight home was uneventful. Sol felt as though he had been gone for a week when Oregon at last appeared beneath them through breaks in the clouds. The barren gold of eastern Oregon, with its rolling sagebrush hills and flats, blended to a line of green where the timber-spiked Cascade Mountains rose to stab the clouds. Sol had a brief glimpse of Mount Hood's snowy base just as the big jet plowed into the clouds draping the western slope of the rocky heights. Just beyond, they began their descent through the gray mass to Portland's runway bordering the river.

At last! Sol sighed. He was nearly home. As the

wheels touched ground he realized he was tired. He had not slept well the night before. They found Perry's car in the parking lot and turned onto the freeway heading south down the Willamette Valley. Forty-five minutes later they were at Perry's house where Sol had left his car. After a quick hello to Vera, Sol drove straight on home, accompanied by the emptiness of failure.

It did not appear that Vic had been to the house. The note still lay on the table where Sol had left it. Tired as he was, he changed into the comfort of his old blue overalls and headed to the barn with a dish of hamburger for Jake. The dog had not been fed since early the morning before.

He'd told Ted to come by before going to work to turn the horses out, but he hadn't thought to ask him to feed Jake. Sol pushed the barn door open and looked in. "Where are you, boy?" he called, glancing toward the corner where Jake usually lay. But there was no sign of the dog. "Here, Jake. Where you hidin', boy?"

Sol called again and again, then stopped, dread clinching to him like a leech. He knew. . . . He knew without knowing. Jake had gone off to die. Did the old dog go to the house first to look for him? he wondered. If so, Sol had not been there to comfort his faithful pal during his last hours.

A lump grew in Sol's throat. He and that old dog had been partners for over fourteen years. "Brought him home in my pocket," he recalled aloud. "Tiny little pup. All warm and squirmy. Whimperin', his milky eyes pleadin' for nothin' but love. Well," Sol gave a heavy sigh, "he was a good pup. A good dog. I thank you, my Friend, for lettin' me have him these past years. Especially this last one since Ruth's been gone."

On the way to the house Sol scraped the hamburger over the pasture fence. Once inside, he dialed Vic's number to see if he was home. The phone was answered on the fourth ring with a slurred "Hello."

"You're home then."

"Got back late last night. Was just taking a nap."

"Sorry to wake you, but I wondered if you'd seen anything of Jake? I can't find him. Thought he might have gone over to your place lookin' for me."

"He wasn't here when I got home," Vic replied. "Hold on a second. I'll look outside." In a moment Vic was back. "I don't see him."

"Most likely then he's gone off to die."

"Well, Dad, he was pretty old for a dog. I'll come over and help you look for him."

They found Jake's stiff body in the tall brown grass beside the chicken coop. He appeared to have been dead for some time. It relieved Sol a little. At least Jake hadn't gone hungry, what with him off in Denver. Together he and Vic buried the dog where they'd found him.

Afterward Vic walked to the house with his father. "I intended on coming over earlier, but then dropped off to sleep in a living-room chair." He chuckled. "Getting just like my father."

Sol eyed his son as they stopped on the back porch to pull their jackets and boots off. "You haven't let up on your drinkin', it appears."

"It's not easy facing that empty house alone."

"I know. Been doin' it for over a year. But drinkin's not gonna help. The emptiness is still right there waitin' when the liquor wears off. Best to face it sober. Live it down day by day. It gets easier with time."

"You've probably never had a drink in your life. How would you know?"

Sol shrugged. "I know. Spent time rebellin' before I met your mother."

With a sigh Vic followed his father into the kitchen. "Had lunch yet?" He glanced at the wall clock above the stove. "It's after two."

"No. And don't start your wet-nursin' me. Thought we were done with all that."

Vic grinned as he sat down at the table. "Then how about *you* making *me* a sandwich?"

"Well now, that's a change." Sol feigned a stern frown. "So, you think it's your turn to be waited on, do you?"

Vic tilted back in the chair, stretched out his legs and asked, "Are you going to be all right, Dad? You thought a lot of that dog. I remember Mom writing how you brought him home to her as a pup. She said she always knew who belonged to Jake, though. She used to send pictures of you and him together. In one I remember you wrestling around with him in the backyard. I. . . ." Vic hesitated before continuing. "I felt a little jealous of that pup, wondering what it would be like to be that close to you."

Sol swallowed around the lump that arose in his throat, and closed his eyes briefly. Guilt hurt, and Sol was hurting enough already. "Didn't have to pretend to be somethin' I wasn't with the dog." A faraway look came to Sol's eyes. "Yes. . . . Jake was a good dog. I'll miss him. Should have had him put down a long time ago, before your mother died. Kept puttin' it off. Then, after she passed on, I couldn't bring myself to do it. It's better for him, now he's gone."

Sol rummaged through the cupboard. He took down a can of bean soup and opened it. He laid out crackers, sliced some cheese, and poured two glasses of milk. He decided Vic needed more nourishment than just coffee. He didn't like the idea of his son's drinking. It wasn't good for him. It wasn't safe, either, driving in that condition. And after Vic had gone on and on about his dad's driving.

The two remained at the table after eating. Vic suggested they find another dog to take Jake's place, but Sol vetoed the idea.

"Don't have the gumption to start over again with another pup. A new dog would be too hard to keep home with so many kids roamin' all over the place. Don't like havin' to keep an animal tied all the time, and never much cared for one in the house. Jake usually stayed on the porch whenever I did let him in."

At last Sol changed the subject. "There's somethin' else we need to talk about."

"Oh, oh. You've got that look again. Now what have I done?"

"Not you. Don't guess you realized, but I was gone all last night."

"You were?" Vic appeared surprised. "You've never cared to be away from home overnight. Where'd you go?"

"Denver. Just got back."

Vic made an effort to keep from smiling. "Sure you did!" Then he took a closer look at his father. "You're not kidding, are you?"

"Nope. Perry went along. It was the first time I'd ever been up in a plane and it nearly scared me to death. Tried not lettin' Perry see how much of a kneeknocker it was for me, so you better not go spillin' it to him."

Sol told Vic the whole of the story from the beginning, starting with Pastor Brock's advice about trying to straighten things out, followed by Vera's marching orders.

When his father finished, Vic inquired "You did all that for me?"

"Did it for Nina as well as you. And for me. Couldn't stand the guilt no longer, knowin' I'd helped bring it all to a head by goin' against Frank the way I did without lettin' you and Nina in on what I'd found out about those guns."

They discussed Frank's reaction to Sol's visit and the possibility of Nina changing her mind and returning after reading the papers Sol had given her.

"That reminds me," Vic said. "A man was at the house early this morning looking for Frank. Said he'd been contacted about some guns Frank had to sell. I told him he was too late. They were already gone. The guy was kind of upset. Wanted to know who bought them, but I played dumb."

Vic turned thoughtful, and went on, "At the time I wondered if you'd made a mistake, letting Frank's ex take them without giving him a chance to tell his side of the dispute. But I see now it was probably best getting them out of here before he turned them into cash. Even if it has locked me in a barrel as far as Nina's concerned. We could have had our tail feathers clipped by the authorities for holding stolen property if that Edgemont woman had pressed charges."

"It put a stop to Frank tryin' to buddy-up with you on that shopping mall, too," Sol added.

"Don't remind me." Vic glanced at his father. "I can't get over your flying clear to Denver to talk to Nina. Even if nothing comes of it, just knowing you tried means a lot, Dad."

Vic appeared more on top of things by the time he left to go home. He hoped, he told Sol, Nina would see through Frank's deceptions now and return. Vic stopped at the back door on his way out. "I think I'll go home and clean the place up—just in case."

Sol was in bed soon after dark that night. Early the next morning he was at the barn when Ted stopped to turn Mike and Bell out. "How was your visit with your friend? I planned to check on you this morning to see if you were back and make sure you were all right," Ted remarked.

"You mean, to see if I was still breathin'?" Sol asked. Then he added, "Jake's dead. Found him yesterday out by the chicken coop."

"Sorry to hear it. I didn't think it would be long, the way he'd been acting." Ted unsnapped Bell's halter, gave the mare a slap on the rump as she backed from her stall, turning to follow Mike out of the barn. "By the way, I'm planning to hitch the horses to the wagon tomorrow. Do you feel up to giving me a hand?"

"Sure. Maybe Vic would help."

"Fine. By the way, have you ever told him you're part owner in these horses?"

Sol shook his head. "Not yet."

That was something else he was going to have to set right. It really wasn't any of Vic's business. It was his own money, after all. Still, it gave him no right to lie about it by concealing the truth.

After Ted left for work Sol walked across the field to Vic's. It seemed odd without Jake following along. It was going to take some getting used to.

Vic opened the door to his father, the morning newspaper in his hand. "I was about to call you." He seemed excited. "Remember the man I told you about? The one who came to buy Frank's guns?"

"Bea Edgemont's guns," Sol corrected as he entered the room.

"There's a story in the paper about him." Vic said, ignoring his father's remark as he flattened the newspaper on the kitchen counter, pushing it in front of Sol. "Right here." He tapped the top of the page with a finger. "It says," Vic began to read over Sol's shoulder, " 'James Morall, wanted nationwide for dealing in illegal arms sales to foreign countries in revolution, was picked up at Portland International Airport after being tipped off by an alert citizen. Authorities, who had been looking for Morall in California and on the East Coast, were puzzled by his unexplained appearance in the Northwest.' "

"Whew!" Sol sat down as his legs turned to mush. "Do you realize what we'd be facin' if Frank had sold those guns to that fella?"

Vic nodded.

"Why don't you cut that piece out and send it to Nina? Tell her that very same man was here the day before askin' for Frank, lookin' to buy Bea's guns."

"I doubt she'd believe me. Probably wouldn't even open the letter."

"It's worth a try. Would give her somethin' to think about."

"It would hurt her, to learn what her father had planned."

"Sometimes we've gotta hurt. Hurtin' brings healin'. I'm gettin' to be quite an authority on that!"

Before heading home, Sol asked Vic if he'd like to help with the horses the next day when Ted hitched them for the first time. Vic said he would. Hoping it sounded like an afterthought, Sol then told Vic how he came to be part owner of the draft team.

"How come you were keeping it a secret? I've wondered why you were so involved with them."

"I didn't want you to know I was takin' charge of

my own life again. You'd been treatin' me like some runny-nosed know-nothin' kid. Like that time you sold my cattle without a word. Haven't much liked things gettin' switched around since you came home. I am the father, after all. And you're still the son."

"I know. I know," Vic admitted. "I've been thinking about that, too. I really don't blame you for feeling the way you do. I had no right taking over. I thought I was helping. Then again, it could be deep down somewhere, without fully realizing it, I was paying you back for ignoring me while I was growing up."

"I'm sorry about your growin' up. More sorry than you'll ever know. But I've tolerated just about all your payback I intend to take."

Vic nodded. "Whenever you want me to do something from now on, Dad, you're going to have to come right out and ask."

14

New Commitments

Saturday morning—the morning of New Year's Eve—Sol awoke to a hard downpour outside his bedroom window. It was the day the blacks were to be hitched for the first time since bringing them home. Sol and Ted had completed repairs on the wagon. The freshly painted tongue was bolted to the front. Ted had replaced the upright crossbars at the front and back of the wagon bed.

Teddy was at the barn with his father and Sol when Vic came over later that morning. The four puttered around as they waited out the weatherman's promised breeze that was supposed to herd the storm clouds on to the east. But the rain continued. While waiting, they brushed and groomed the animals and greased the wagon wheels. Everything was set to go—everything except for the weather.

Sol was buckling Bell's harness in place while Ted adjusted Mike's in the next stall. "Come look at this. I've had to let this strap out around her midsection again."

"We did that just the other day," Ted commented, placing a hand on Bell's solid rump as he came around behind the mare. "She *must* be carrying a foal."

"Did you ever write their former owner to find out

what stud she was bred to if she does pitch us a foal one of these days?"

"Not yet. But I will."

With the harnessing completed, Vic pulled the wide double doors closed and drew up a couple bales of hay in front of the horse stalls. "Might as well sit and get comfortable. It's not too cold in here as long as the doors are shut."

"It's sure been a wet winter so far," Ted noted. "It's not easy getting used to."

"I miss the snow we had back in Iowa," Teddy grumbled.

"Reminds me of a December we had some sixty years back," Sol began. They listened as Sol yarned, then prodded him to tell more. Spurred on by Vic's interest, Sol continued through several more stories.

Vic then asked Ted more about the draft-horse hobby that was getting a foothold around the country. Sol took the occasion to mention he'd finally let Vic in on the partnership they'd struck with the horses. Ted appeared relieved to have it out in the open at last.

Teddy grew tired of sitting, and climbed the ladder to the loft. They could hear him thumping and banging about overhead. "Hey," he called down, "what are you going to do with these broken crates, Sol? They're empty."

"Don't rightly know. Have to clean 'em out of there one of these days."

"Can I have the boards if I get 'em down?"

"Sure. Go to it."

Ted groaned. "Do you have any idea what our garage is going to look like with Teddy's building projects strung all over?"

At noon May brought them sandwiches and a thermos of hot soup. The rain still gave no promise of letting up. After eating the men helped Teddy lower the boards from the loft. Ted then backed his stock truck inside so they could load the boards and haul them over to his garage. Sol and Vic rode along to help with the unloading.

Sol had not ventured onto his former farmland since it had become a housing development; land where he'd once raised corn, alfalfa, and strawberries. It was a whole different world there now. A sense of loss pricked him as he recalled the peace he'd experienced working his fields.

Youngsters were idly circling their bikes in the middle of the street, defying the rain. They did not appear to be the ruffians he had envisioned. Maybe, he thought, if he got to know them—as he had Teddy—and they got to know him, they would not be so prone to mischief on his property.

Standing out of the rain in the gaping doorway of Ted's garage, looking up and down the street as the others began unloading boards from the truck, Sol ventured, "We ought to drive the team and wagon over sometime, Ted. The kids around here would probably get a kick out of a hayride."

Vic and Ted stopped in their tracks, their arms a tangled with boards. Neither made a comment, although Vic was smiling as he returned to the truck for another load.

"Sounds good to me," Ted commented sober-faced. "I've thought about it, but didn't figure you'd go for the idea."

Looking a trifle sheepish, Sol admitted, "It's kind of selfish, I guess. Thought it might slow the vandalism over at my place."

At last, with the rain falling even heavier, they gave

up hitching the horses that day. Ted drove Vic and Sol back to the farm, where they turned the horses loose. "Maybe tomorrow," he called hopefully as he ran through the storm to his truck.

"Well. . . ." Vic appeared at a loss. He turned to his father. "How about coming home with me? I've got a couple steaks in the refrigerator."

Sol stood in the barn doorway gazing out at the rain. "Can do my own cookin', thank you. Been doin' fine lately."

"I wasn't implying you *needed* someone to cook for you. I'd like you to come over." Vic turned away in disgust. "You'll never change. You're as feisty an old crust as ever!"

Looking around, Sol blustered, "And don't you go forgettin' it either! I've had enough of you makin' me feel old and of no account. It's true I wasn't doin' so good when you first came back last year. But instead of helpin', you kept shovin' me down. Why, I could have another good ten years left. Don't intend rockin' it away."

A scowl shadowed Vic's face. "I give up. You'll never change! I thought we were beginning to understand one another." He shook his head as he started for the door, then stopped, tempering his words with, "Dad, if I admit you're partly right, will you admit that maybe I am, too?"

"Already told you that," Sol said.

Vic smiled, feigning a slight bow. "Dad. I'd very much like it if you'd join me for dinner tonight. As my guest."

"Supper," Sol corrected.

"Dinner, supper, whatever. Will you come? I. . . ." He stopped, taking a measured breath. "I don't want to be alone tonight. I guess what I'm saying is, I *need* your company. Especially tonight. It was New Year's Eve when I first asked Nina out."

Sol felt an impulse to reach out and put an arm around this man who had at one time been his little boy. Holding himself in check, Sol merely shrugged. "Might go over. For a while anyway."

Later, after their meal, Sol helped Vic clean up the kitchen. Vic was muttering. "Guess I'd better run the dishwasher."

"You talkin' to me or to yourself?" Sol inquired.

"Been alone too much lately," Vic admitted. "Find myself talking aloud to myself just like you've always done."

"Don't talk to myself."

"Not much you don't! You've always talked to yourself."

"Not me I talk to."

"Then just who might it be?"

"God. I've always talked things over with God."

"When did you become so religious? You seldom went to church when I was growing up."

"Didn't say I was religious," Sol countered. "It's a bit more than that." He handed Vic the last dirty dish from the counter. "I'm real sorry about not goin' to church with you and Janet and your mother. Was always a loner. Figured I could worship God on my own terms, in my own way, as well or better than at church. But I see now I missed out on a lot by not goin' with you."

Vic stared at his father. Water dripped from his hands onto the floor. "I just took it for granted you didn't believe in God. I stopped going to church, if you'll remember, when I was in junior high, deciding if you didn't need it, neither did I."

"I was afraid it had been somethin' like that." Slowly Sol straightened his shoulders, noting with a gruffness he did not feel, "Then it's high time you started back. I went last Sunday mornin'. Plan on goin' again tomorrow. Better come with me."

"*You* went to church?" Vic stared at his father, finally adding, "I might go sometime. But not tomorrow."

The rain kept up all night. By morning it had diminished to a light drizzle with the sky showing bright streaks along the western horizon. Sol called Ted, wishing him a Happy New Year and telling him he was going to church, but would be ready to help with the horses that afternoon if the clouds cleared away.

"Church?" Ted inquired. "I didn't know you went to church."

"What's the matter with everybody? People *do* still go to church, you know."

"I'm sorry," Ted soothed. "It's just that I had no idea you ever went."

"Haven't much since I was a boy. Started back last Sunday. How about you and the family comin' along with me?"

"We used to go when we lived in Iowa," Ted admitted. "Got out of the habit after moving here. Come to think of it, it might be just what Kathy needs. What our whole family needs."

"Well then, come along," Sol said. Then he told him which church he was attending.

"The kids would probably feel more comfortable in the denomination we're used to."

Sol felt good as he hung up the phone. He had never been able to express himself about such things before. Ruth was the one who could talk right out about her faith. "Thank you, Lord, for helpin' me have my say with Ted and Vic."

When Sol walked in through the church door later, he felt more at ease than he had the Sunday before. He nodded to some he knew and to others he recalled meeting, although he could not remember their names. Pastor Brock expounded on "God, the Forgiver." Later, Sol found his spirits lifting as he drove home. He had received on invitation to a church pot-luck the following week, but he had refused to commit himself.

By two o'clock the rain had stopped and the sun was poking through the clouds. Ted and Teddy drove in about the same time as Vic. Teddy raced to the barn and found that Sol already had the horses in and rubbed dry.

He was wiping the harness down when Teddy thundered in through the side door. "We're gonna do it, Sol. We're gonna do it this time!"

Sol grinned. "Looks that way."

Vic tried helping with the harness, but gave up. "I didn't realize there was so much to it," he commented, standing back to watch with Teddy. "Don't see how you remember which strap goes where."

With the harness fastened in place, Ted and Sol led the horses out to the waiting hay wagon, stepping them around with one on either side of the wagon tongue. Vic went to the front to hold Mike while Teddy held onto Bell. Sol and Ted fastened the lines to the horses' bits, running them back through rings on the hames that were snugged in against the collars. The neck yoke was then snapped to the front, securing the animals together. Sol lifted the wagon tongue and pulled it through a larger ring centered on the neck yoke as Ted went around to hook the traces to the doubletree. They were ready.

"I think," Sol said to Ted, "you'd better try them in

the field first. It's been a long time since they've been driven. We never did see them pull anything."

Ted nodded. "I was thinking that same thing. Why don't you and Vic walk on either side until we get through the gate. It should be soft enough out there, what with all the rain we've had, to slow them if they decide to run."

Mike tossed his head in anticipation while Bell maintained her usual calm. Ted climbed up on the wagon, bracing himself against the front crossbars.

"Can I come?" Teddy begged.

"Not yet. I'd better take them around a time or two alone."

"Don't forget, they'll sense it if you're nervous," Sol reminded him.

Ted nodded. "I know. Well," he took a deep breath, "here goes."

Mike lunged ahead as Vic put a steadying hand on the big gelding's neck. "Easy there, boy," he crooned.

Bell bowed her massive neck, stepping out easily as Sol walked beside her. Mike swung his head, nipping at her but missed, his long teeth snapping air. The mare laid her ears back, warning him with a swing of her own head as the wagon rolled effortlessly on its rubber-tired wheels through the gate and out onto the spongy field, slicing deeply into the saturated sod. Mike, brought into line by Bell's threatened retaliation, calmed some.

"Okay," Ted nodded. "Let me try them alone."

Sol stopped, allowing the wagon to roll on past. Vic did the same on the opposite side as Teddy ran up to stand between them.

"You don't think they'll run away with Dad, do you, Sol?"

With Vic's hand on the boy's shoulder, he assured

him, "No. Of course they won't. Your dad will soon have them under control."

But Sol was not so sure. Mike was dancing a jig, his legs pumping like feathered pistons, striking the ground three times to every one of Bell's strides. Ted swung them in a tight circle, forcing Mike on the outside while keeping Bell in check toward the center.

Teddy was pulling on Sol's arm. "Dad can hold them if they run, can't he?"

"Sure!" Sol declared, hoping he was right.

Just then Mike reared, jerking Bell hard in against him.

"Come on! Ted needs help," Sol shouted as he broke into a stiff run.

The gelding came down with his right front leg over the wagon tongue. By the time Sol reached them Ted was on the ground holding Mike by the bridle. The big horse, his eyes wild, stood on three legs, his body leaning crazily toward the outside.

Before Vic could think of what to do, his father had run in jabbing his shoulder hard into Mike's chest. The horse grunted, leaning back, his leg forced up and nearly over the tongue. Sol made a grab for the hoof and hung on.

"Vic! Give a hand!"

Bending low under the horse's neck, Vic grasped the hoof with his father, pulling it up and over the tongue. Mike's platter-sized hoof slapped the ground, spattering them with mud. Sol stepped back to get his breath, placing a hand on Bell's neck to steady himself.

"You okay, Dad?" Vic asked.

Sol nodded.

Ted ran his hand down Mike's leg. For once the gelding stood stock-still, only his ears in motion. "He seems okay."

"We'd better take them to the barn," Vic suggested.

Ted shook his head. "Can't do that. Not now. Mike will do this every time he's hitched if we quit now. I've got to drive them."

With Sol in agreement, Ted took up the lines and climbed back on the wagon. Mike didn't offer to move. As Ted coaxed the team ahead, Bell readily stepped out. But Mike hung back. Ted flipped him with the end of a line. The horse flinched, then lunged forward before settling down to a mincing walk beside his teammate.

After several minutes Vic commented, "They do look good in harness, don't they?"

"Yah," Teddy breathed. "Gives me goose bumps even though they scare me sometimes."

"They should be all right now," Sol noted. "Mike's found he can't get by with his foolishness."

"Man!" Vic said with a shake of his head. "They *are* beauties!"

Glancing at his son, Sol remarked, "I do think you're catchin' it."

"Catching what?"

"Horse fever."

Vic smiled, without taking his eyes from the blacks as they sloshed over the soft, rain sogged field.

By the time Ted completed two full rounds, the horses were sweating, but walking steadily as though they had been hitched every day. Ted finally pulled to a stop to let his audience climb aboard.

Steam rose from the animals' backs later as they were unhitched to be led to the barn. Mike rubbed his head on Vic's shoulder, nearly knocking the man off his feet.

After the horses were in their stalls, their harness pulled off, and they were wiped down, Vic said to Ted,

"I'd like to drive them sometime."

Ted smiled. "Sure, why not? How about next weekend? If it's not raining."

Sol's shoulder ached where he'd rammed it into Mike's chest. He rubbed it, a feeling of satisfaction easing over him. He'd risen to the emergency right well for a man who'd thought his life was over a while back.

After the Bowens left, Vic walked to the house with his father. "That was pretty swift thinking, Dad. You were moving real good out there. I had no idea what to do." He slapped his father on the back.

"Kinda proud of myself," Sol admitted a bit sheepishly.

As they neared the house, Vic commented, "I miss that old dog not being around."

"I do too. It's helped havin' so much goin' on lately."

Sol glanced at his son as they went into the house. "How are you gettin' along without Nina?"

Vic sighed, and followed his father into the kitchen. "I miss her more than I ever thought I could miss anyone."

"Still no word?"

"Nothing. I tried calling after you'd been to see her, but she still wouldn't come to the phone."

"Thought by now she'd have seen through Frank, especially after I gave her those papers."

Sol did not voice his next thought. Maybe she never would come back. "Well, we've got us a brand-new year to try to work things out. With the good Lord's help, we'll come through no matter what's thrown our way."

A hint of a smile creased Vic's face. "Seems to me you and I have already come some distance, Dad."

15

Hayride to Healing

With the new year before him, Sol decided he would look ahead instead of back. He had been keeping one eye on the calendar ever since Ruth passed on, reminding himself over and over again: "Last year at this time Ruth and I were. . ." But that year, that first awful mixed-up year, was behind him. He had no idea what lay ahead, and yet he felt himself ready to meet whatever it was face-on, rather than humped with his back to the storm. And so it was with renewed vigor that Sol marched into the year, cutting a path for himself without his wife, after almost giving up.

While his concern over the breakup of his son's marriage continued to pinch his conscience, it was not enough of a pinch to raise a blister, or smother his newfound—What was it? Peace? Yes, he decided, it was that and more.

His deeper commitment to the Lord God as the great and mighty King, as well as Sol's own special Friend and Companion, took root from the seed of his desperation. An extended vision of God had brought hope and a sense of expectancy. A quiet joy buoyed him now, in spite of the dismal graying of winter that hung tough to the land. As the Denver-bound plane had propelled him beyond the clouds into the brilliance of the sun, so his spirit sought the energizing light and warmth of an even greater Son.

He smiled more. He caught himself humming now and then. He was becoming a regular at church on Sunday mornings, and sometimes even for Wednesday evening Bible study. He had gone to several social functions. Ruth, he decided, would hardly know him when he finally crossed that invisible line separating his world from hers. There he would one day soon (although he was not in so much of a rush as before) be with her again, at last meeting his Lord and Savior face-to-face.

The Marshes invited Sol and Vic to town for dinner a couple of times. The four talked and laughed, recalling humorous times from the past when their farms were in operation. It was good including Ruth in conversation with people who had known her so well. Some folks, Sol found, went out of their way to change the subject whenever he mentioned his deceased wife, ignoring Ruth's existence as though she had never walked the earth or been a part of his life. He realized they did it for his sake, not wishing to strike a match to his loss. What they did not understand was that he wanted, needed, and yearned to talk about her.

The one shadow still dogging him was Vic's despair over Nina. She had accepted Vic's letter with the news story of the arrest of James Morall and sent a short note in reply. While she had evidently not locked the door on their marriage, she appeared reluctant to return, using the excuse that she needed more time. Sol was afraid that was not a good sign, but, he reasoned, there was nothing more he could do about it.

As time drew Sol further back from the picture, it gave him a better view of the whole. He had been right in letting Bea take those guns. Her guns. Even if his handling of the affair had been flawed.

Frank would no doubt have sold them, turning Bea's innocent collection into illegal contraband meant to kill and maim. Even if he, Vic, and Frank had escaped arrest along with Morall, Frank would no doubt have continued prodding Vic into exiling his father to a retirement home. Yes, it was hard to tell just what would have come of them all if Frank had not been stopped. And, although Sol knew it was wrong, he could not help feeling some pride for his part in boxing Frank into a corner.

After trying to smooth things over between Vic and Nina, he could think of nothing more to do. There was no sense beating himself to death over a matter out of his control, he decided. He continued to pray for them. The Lord was perfectly capable of straightening things out in his own good time.

Sol well remembered how long it had taken his own wounds to begin the healing process after suddenly being left alone. He sympathized with his son. While Sol had no chance of ever seeing Ruth again this side of death's invisible barrier, Vic could still hope, dim though it was, for Nina's return. At least it appeared Vic had stopped his excessive drinking, for which Sol thanked his Lord.

The sky remained clear more often as April arrived wrapped in lush greens and pastel blossoms, escorting spring to the valley of Oregon's Willamette River. As with the seasons of earth, so the reclamation from the wintering of Sol's soul continued. A renewed hope in the future, for both himself and his son, surged strong within him as he took note of pussy willows and dogwoods in bloom along the roadside on his trips to town.

He was meeting Perry nearly every morning now for coffee and donuts at a local cafe on the outskirts of town. His friend had become a regular there since moving to town, joining other retirees, men who gathered to jaw, work out the world's ailments, and keep the waitresses on their toes.

Vic and Sol had both driven the horses on the wagon by that time. Teddy had even had a chance at the lines after Mike learned he could not get away with bullying them no matter how big or bad he proved himself to be. Sol derived more pleasure from watching Vic handle the team than in driving them himself.

It was a bright sunlit Saturday when they finally got around to taking the subdivision youngsters for a hayride. Sol and Teddy tossed hay bales on the wagon while Vic helped Ted harness and hitch the team.

Sol cut the twine on the bales and shook out enough hay to cover the wagon bed. "Do the kids know we're comin'?" he asked the boy.

"I told some of the guys," Teddy said. "They don't believe you'll come with us, though."

"They don't think old Grumps has it in him, huh?" Sol inquired with a smile.

Ready and rolling, Sol stood at the front of the wagon, holding onto the crossbars as Ted swung the horses out of the driveway onto the blacktop. Vic was on the other side of Ted. Teddy lay on his back in the hay watching scattered clouds overhead change shape in the fathomless blue of the sky.

Ted turned the team down the first street leading into the development. The horses' shoeless hooves clopped in rhythm on the pavement. As they made a swing around the first long block of homes, people peered out through windows, around corners, from under car hoods, and from open garages. Ted pulled the team to a stop every now and then, motioning them to climb aboard for a ride. More adults than children accepted their invitation at first.

"Hi, Teddy," a boy called scrambling on the wagon at one stop. He noticed Sol then, and eyed the man warily.

On down the street several more youngsters were gathered in a knot watching their approach. They walked hesitantly to the wagon when Ted stopped and motioned them to come along.

"What's the catch?" one boy, a bit older and taller than the rest, demanded.

Sol reached out a hand. "No catch. Here, I'll help you up."

The boy just stood there, his hands thrust in the pockets of a bright yellow windbreaker. Sol was sure he had seen that same windbreaker on a boy running through his orchard the week before. The other boys stayed behind their older companion.

"Oh, come on," Sol urged. "I don't bite. At least not hard or often."

"How come you stopped for *us*?" another inquired, belligerence shading his voice.

Sol straightened. "Why shouldn't we?" He gestured toward those already on the wagon. "Thought it might be a neighborly thing to do. Can you think of any reason why we wouldn't want you boys along?"

All but the taller one shook their heads.

"Then come on." Sol reached down again and helped them up one by one. The older boy ignored Sol's offer of aid, going instead to the back of the wagon. He hopped up to settle himself in the hay behind a couple of women, arms encircling his knees. The other boys clustered around the front with Teddy, asking questions about the horses.

Ted urged the team on again and made the rounds

of the twisted streets, some people getting off while others clambered on. Sol became concerned about the wagon bearing the weight. It did, although the team had to get down to the business of pulling a few times on the sight inclines. Teddy's friends were still on board when they neared the Bowens' house. The yellow-jacketed boy had inched toward the front as Sol explained how he had used just such a wagon to haul loose hay to the barn before buying his first hay baler.

Ted's wife came out to join them as Ted pulled Mike and Bell to a stop in front of the house. Kathy was in the driveway standing beside a low slung metallic-blue Ford. She was talking to some teenagers in the car, a girl and two boys. Kathy deliberately turned her back on the wagon at the curb, while those in the car craned their necks for a better view.

"Come on, Kathy," Sol called to the girl. "Bring your friends and come for a ride."

She shook her head without looking around.

The car doors suddenly started popping open and the three teenagers scrambled out to head for the wagon.

"Sounds good to me," the driver of the car remarked.

Slowly Kathy turned, wooden and unyielding, as her friends deserted her to scramble on the already overloaded hay wagon.

"Come on, Kathy," Sol urged. "You could probably talk your dad into lettin' you drive. He tells me you used to be a pretty fair horsewoman."

She shook her head.

"Oh, come on, Kathy," her girlfriend called. "It'll be fun!"

"Yah," the first boy encouraged. "How come you

didn't tell us your dad had a team of big horses and a wagon like this?"

"Didn't think anyone would care," she muttered, reluctantly walking toward them and climbing on the wagon with the others. She flopped down in the hay. Her face flushed as her eyes nearly connected with Sol's.

After another turn around the development they delivered everyone back to their homes. Teddy's young friends hopped off close to where they had been picked up. They shouted their thanks as they raced toward a nearby house, except for yellow jacket, who remained silently glum as he trailed the others with a pronounced swagger.

Ted turned the horses back to his own house, where Kathy and her friends piled off. "Thanks a lot, Mr. Bowen," the three teens chorused as they walked to their car. The driver looked back. "You wouldn't want to trade vehicles, would you? Might even be persuaded to throw in my new sound system."

Everyone but Kathy laughed.

Ted handed the lines to Vic. "Why don't you and your dad drive them back alone. I'll have May bring me over to help unhitch pretty soon."

"Think we can handle it, Dad?" Vic asked.

Sol nodded. "Why not! You're gettin' to be a pretty fair teamster for an old oil man."

With Vic at the lines they rolled effortlessly along the paved road toward the tall white farmhouse towering over the smaller development dwellings like a white leghorn hen watching over a brood of multi-hued chicks. Mike blew threw his nose and tossed his head, eager to reach the barn. Bell bowed her thick neck and trotted beside the light-stepping gelding with the heavy complacency of a mother-in-waiting.

The wagon's rubber tires swished along the pavement as the eight platter-sized hooves beat out a rhythm known to travelers down through the centuries.

"I get a kick out of driving them," Vic remarked. "Have you and Ted ever thought about buying another team? We could put a four-horse hitch together."

"Yep," said Sol, "It's happened."

"What's happened?"

"You've caught it."

Vic smiled. "Oh. You mean horse fever?"

Sol nodded. "The way I figure, it won't be long before Bell puts a foal on the ground. If we have her bred right back, we'd have ourselves another team in three or four years." Sol chuckled. "May seem like a long time off to you, like I might not be around to see it. But I have a feelin' I've got some good years left."

"It's helped having the horses to work with, hasn't it?"

Sol nodded again.

Pulling on the lines to steady Mike, Vic noted, "I know it's helped me, working with you and the horses since Nina left."

He glanced at his father. "Have I ever told you the reason my first marriage ended?"

"No, you never did. Figured it was none of my business."

"I've had a feeling you thought Nina broke Beth and me up. But the truth is Beth started seeing someone else. I was gone a lot, so I guess it was partly my own fault. I felt something was wrong a year before Beth checked out of our marriage. It didn't come as any great surprise when she told me she was getting a divorce.

"I met Nina a couple months later. We felt it was right for us from the start, even though there is a fifteen-year difference in our ages. I care about that woman, Dad. I thought she felt the same about me." He smiled, shook his head and worked his hands further down on the lines. "I understand more now—how you felt when you lost Mom."

But Sol was not listening. He was staring at something. Someone was standing at the end of his driveway. Sol pointed. "Wonder who that could be? Looks a little like. . . ."

"It's Nina!" Vic declared, slapping lines to the horses. Sol grabbed for a crossbar to keep his feet under him as the wagon jerked ahead.

Nina was waving.

Sol glanced toward the barn, then the house. There was no sign of a car. Or of Frank.

Cupping her hands to her mouth, the young woman called to them as the wagon slowed, "How about a ride?"

Vic pulled the team in, looking down in disbelief. Nina was wearing jeans and a ski-type, pink quilted jacket. Her pink-and-white tennis shoes were caked with mud, evidence she had walked across the field from Vic's place. A breeze blew the dark hair back from her face as she stood looking up at Vic and her father-in-law.

"I tried calling as soon as my plane landed. I finally took a bus to town, then a taxi on out here, after getting no answer from either place."

"How long are you planning to stay?" Vic inquired.

Her smile faded. "I didn't intend on leaving again. I mean, if that's all right with you."

"Oh!" Sol was growing impatient with the two. "Of course it's all right with him. With me, too."

Vic nodded. "I've missed you."

"And I've missed you."

192

Stepping to the edge of the wagon, Sol reached down. "Then get on up here so you two can start patchin' things together."

May drove in with Ted as they reached the barn. "Go along with you," Sol said, giving Vic a push. "Ted and I can manage without you."

After Ted left, Sol walked to the house alone, glancing heavenward. "My Friend, I thank you for bringin' Nina back. Guess I'm about as grateful as a man can be. But now," Sol sighed, "you're gonna need to help me learn this father-in-lawin' bit. Won't be easy, I'm thinkin'. Too set in my ways. Still don't know that much about bein' a father." Sol had to smile. "Only you could soften an old coot like me."

He did not see much of Vic for several days. Whenever his son did venture over, he was always alone and anxious to get back to his wife. He seemed happy. Sol asked him to bring Nina along sometime, but Vic usually found an excuse about her being busy or having some place to go.

When Sol returned from his morning coffee break with Perry a few days after Nina's return, he walked over to Vic's house. Nina, however, immediately found something that needed attention in another part of the house. He didn't need to be stepped on like a crunched bug to realize she was avoiding him. After all, hadn't he avoided her when Vic first brought her to Oregon? Sol knew all the tricks. Well, he figured, he probably had it coming. At least things were better between her and Vic. Maybe that was all he could ever hope for.

It was a Wednesday afternoon when Vic phoned to deliver some disturbing news. "Frank's coming back. Due in tomorrow morning. Nina's gone after groceries. Thought I'd better warn you while she was out."

Sol decided to open the subject of Nina's coolness toward him. At first Vic laughed it off, but then admitted it was true. "You've got to remember, Frank *is* her father. No one enjoys being forced to admit their father is up to no good or involved in shady deals. Even if deep down they realize it's true."

Dread settled over Sol again as he contemplated Frank's return. Why would the man want to come back? It took guts. Would he try making trouble for Vic and Nina again? Sol was not exactly afraid of Frank, but neither did he look forward to seeing the man again.

Bell's time to foal was drawing near. All doubts ceased when her milk bag began to swell. Sol decided to concentrate on the imminent arrival of the foal rather than working himself into a lather over Frank. He had prayed about it. He would leave the outcome in the Lord's hands.

Both Ted and Sol kept a close eye on the mare. Ted had finally received a reply from the shires' former owner. It was a Percheron stud, a tall leggy black, that got in with the mares before the team was sold.

Sol went to work on the other two horse stalls, tearing out the center divider to make a box stall large enough for the mare and foal. He was spreading clean straw on the wood-plank floor on Friday morning when the barn door creaked open. Sol straightened to see who it was, then bent back to his work.

"I see you're still keeping busy out here at the barn."

Sol made no reply as he forked a wad of straw into a corner. The sound of footsteps had stopped on the other side of the partition.

"I told Vic I wanted to talk to you alone," Frank said. "Is it all right? My coming over like this, I mean?"

"Space above ground's free to fill with whatever you've a mind to, including any hot air you might be peddlin'."

"I didn't come to argue. Or cause trouble. I wanted to apologize for the way I acted when you were at my sister's house. I had no cause to order you out."

"No need worryin' it around none. What's done is done. Nina's back where she belongs. Bea's got what's hers again. And I've still got what belongs to me. As they say, all's well that ends well." Sol straightened to look at the puffy-cheeked man, his glare hard and unyielding.

Frank never flinched. "You're right. Things finally turned out all right for the rest of you. I'd like to do something to make amends, but I don't know what."

"You could leave," Sol suggested, his tone flat. "Leave Vic and Nina alone. Just go away."

"I can't. I'm broke, Sol. Flat-out broke. I'm not old enough for social security. I've got no income. No home."

"Now whose fault is that?" Sol demanded.

"Mine," Frank agreed without hesitation. "It's mine."

Without another word the man turned and walked out of the barn, closing the door softly behind him. Sol stood there staring at the back side of the plank door. "Well, my Friend. Has the worm turned color, or. . . ." For some reason Sol could not bring himself to swallow the scene he'd just played a part in. "Somethin's not as it appears," he decided aloud.

Frank stayed on for several days, then left only to return a week later. Sol asked Vic what was going on, but Vic didn't seem to want to talk about it or Frank. Sol could tell his son was uncomfortable with the subject.

Then one evening Nina called to invite Sol to dinner the following night. Taken completely off guard, Sol replied, "Afraid I can't. Goin' to a potluck the senior citizen bunch is havin' at church. I do thank you, though, for the invite."

"Why don't you stop by later," she persisted. "On your way home. I'm baking a pie."

Sol was pleased with Nina's friendly tone, so pleased he came close to agreeing to pass on the church potluck. But he didn't. Frank would be there. And yet he longed for a healing between them all. At last he agreed to stop by the house on his way home.

With a sigh Sol hung up the receiver. "Gonna need all the help you can send my way, my Friend."

The following evening Sol emptied a couple cans of pork and beans into one of Ruth's baking dishes and placed it in the oven. He made a last check on Bell before driving to the church fellowship hall, where about twenty people had gathered to share the meal. A good many were widows, but Sol was not interested. There would only be one woman in his life. He did enjoy himself, though. They were a friendly lot. Several who had known Ruth talked to him about her, which he appreciated.

On the way home it nearly slipped his mind that he was expected at Vic and Nina's place. Sol remembered just before turning into his own driveway and so he drove on to their house. He noticed the living-room drapes were open as he got out of his car. From the darkness Sol could see Frank standing in the middle of the room talking, his arms and hands gesturing whatever point he was trying to make.

Sol was of a mind to get back in his car and go on home. But, he decided, they had probably heard him.

As he hesitated he saw Nina get up and cross the room to the front door.

He sighed. "Well, here goes nothin', Lord."

16

Sol Takes Charge

"I thought I heard a car out here," Nina called from the open doorway as she flipped the porch switch on, stabbing the darkness with light. "I was afraid you'd changed your mind." Her tone seemed genuine.

Sol entered the living room, nodding to Vic, who rose without a word from the couch to face his father. Directing a slight tucking of the head in Frank's general vicinity without actually looking at the man, Sol took note of the fire behind the two, hungrily lapping at oak logs within the deep recesses of the white marble hearth.

"Evenin'," Sol greeted.

The three men sat down, with Sol choosing a place beside Vic at the opposite end of the couch. Nina fussed as Sol knew women were prone to do at such times, carrying in a tray from the kitchen with thick wedges of coconut cream pie and mugs of strong black coffee. Vic remained quiet—unusually quiet, Sol decided. Frank adjusted his bulk to a deep-cushioned chair directly across from Sol, a glass-topped coffee table between them. A running battery of words spilled from Frank as he hunched over his plate, talking as he chewed. The atmosphere was definitely strained. Sol not only sensed it; he felt it. Whatever it was had doused the warmth from the room, reducing the cheery snap of the fire to hollow, crackling echoes.

Sol ate in silence, tuning out Frank's ceaseless prattle while silently pleading with God—for what? What had he walked into? he wondered.

Nina came into the room again from the kitchen. "Dad's going back overseas. This is a good-bye for him tonight," she said, directing her attention to Sol.

He glanced at her, carefully laying the fork across his empty pie plate, which he placed on the coffee table in front of him. Nina crossed the room to sit on the arm of the couch beside Vic, her arm resting on her husband's shoulder.

Frank leaned forward. "Yep, got my old job back."

"Thought they weren't lettin' Americans back in that country," Sol remarked.

"They're not. At least not many. The company Vic and I worked for," Frank offered a thin, strained smile in Vic's direction, "the one we both thought we'd retired from, is asking for volunteers. They're hoping to smooth things over so they can get back in operation. They've offered a pretty fair wage for the effort."

"But the risk, Dad," Nina stressed. "Nothing's worth that!"

"It is if you've got no other way to make a living." Frank avoided Sol's gaze. "I'm too old to land a decent job here in the States, at least one that pays anything. The investments I sank my savings into went under. There doesn't seem to be anything left for me here."

Sol glanced at Vic to find him turned away, staring into the fire, absenting himself from the conversation.

"Can't you talk Dad out of this, Vic?" Nina prodded.

"He knows what he's getting into."

Sol straightened, clearing his throat. "When you leavin'?" Regretting his thinly disguised delight with the man's planned departure, Sol added, "There must be some way to earn an *honest* living here in this country."

Frank rested his elbows on his knees. "There is. But you've already vetoed my—I mean, the best opportunity any of us will ever have."

"*I* did? Must have missed somethin'?"

"Sol, if we were to go ahead with that shopping center it would stake us all." Frank was absentmindedly rubbing his palms together. "I have a natural ability for putting deals like that together. If you and Vic could just get the center built, I know I could run a successful promotion to lease the spaces. Why, we'd have potential buyers lined up to take it off our hands. The area around here is growing. There's no stopping it. Someone's going to build a shopping center if we don't."

"Not on my land, they're not! At least not while I'm still breathin'." Sol's eyes narrowed to slits. So, this was why he'd been invited. He turned to Vic, who was now watching his father.

"And just what have you to say about all this?" Sol demanded.

"Not much." Vic's tone was one of restrained amusement.

"Vic!" Nina pleaded.

"No, honey. I'm not going to talk Dad into doing something against his better judgment. I'll not be a party to that again."

"Sol." Frank scooted forward, reaching across the coffee table to grasp the older man's wrist. "A shopping center would be a natural out here. The first one, the only one, in this area. We couldn't help but make money. Think of it."

"I am thinkin'. I'm thinkin' you don't have a thing to lose." Sol pulled free from Frank's grip. "Not your land. Not your money. Nothin'. All you're lookin' for is to ride Vic and me straight to the bank. You say you've lost money on some bad investments. Don't sound like you've made such good business moves up to now. What makes think you're such a whoop-de-do of a business manager, anyway?"

Frank paled. "It's not the same. Public relations. Now that's a gift. *My* gift. I know I can swing it. For all of us."

"Public relations." Sol rolled the words on his tongue, his eyes searching the ceiling where fire shadows swayed in silent dance. "I would imagine the tools of that trade have been used by every con man sittin' behind bars today."

Invisible barriers of silence sectioned off the room, entrapping the four within their own spheres.

At last Vic slowly got to his feet and stood beside his wife, who remained on the arm of the couch. His hand grasped her shoulder as her eyes remained downcast. "I'm sorry, honey, but I can't stand by like this any longer. I know you're hurting over your father leaving. But I won't sell *my* father down the tube to keep Frank here. I can't do that."

Nina nodded, a tear slipping from an eye. Pain etched her face as she slowly looked up at Sol. "I'm sorry, Father Timins. It's just that I. . . . It's so dangerous over there."

"I know," Sol acknowledged, hauling himself up off the couch. "But there's nothin' I can do about it. Guess I'd better be goin' on home. I thank you for the pie."

He started for the door, then stopped and turned deliberately toward Frank. "I'm sorry for you, Frank. You've got a daughter here to be proud of. And yet it appears you've been tryin' to use her to get your hands on somethin' that's not yours. If you do go overseas, I wish you well. But remember, I've had nothin' whatever to do with your predicament, and so feel no responsibility to carry you along on my back."

At the door Sol turned again. "Frank, why don't you quit feedin' on other folks? Stand on your own feet for a change. Those the Good Lord gave you. He never intended us to tramp around on others the way you've been doin'." Sol opened the door and stepped out into the comforting darkness, calling back, "Good night, all."

"Sol!" Frank came to the door, spreading his hands before him in a pleading gesture. "I don't know *how* to make it on my own!"

"Then," Vic broke in from behind him, "I'd say it was high time you learned, Frank."

"I'm too old!"

"No, you're not," Sol told him as Vic switched the porch light on. "I'm still learnin' at my age. Couldn't have done it without the Lord, though. You might think on that. Give God a try, Frank. Just remember, though, he's not one you can con."

The next day Vic was at Sol's place early and tried to explain away the happenings of the night before, but Sol was in no mood to hear it. "All I care," he told his son, "was that you finally backed me. For that I thank you."

"I told Frank I wouldn't try talking you into going ahead with the mall. But I did agreed to let him have his say. I was sure you wouldn't go for it. In fact, I was counting on you turning him down. One thing we don't need right now is to get involved with Frank in some kind of deal. For Nina's sake I've offered to fly to Texas with him to look into that job."

"She goin' along?"

Vic shook his head. "No. I'll only be gone a couple days."

"When you leavin'?"

"Tomorrow morning. Early. Would you mind going over to see her while I'm gone? On top of Frank leaving, she's upset over what happened last night. He's been working on her, wearing her down, trying to get us both to side with him on building the mall."

Sol nodded. "I'll talk to her. Not sure what good it will do." He sighed. "But I'll give it a try."

Vic placed a hand on his father's arm. "Thanks, Dad. I don't want to risk losing her again."

The next day Sol found himself actually feeling sorry for Frank. He called Perry to tell him what had taken place.

"Let's be praying for the man," Perry noted at the other end of the line. "Sounds like you told him what needed to be said."

"I'd sure appreciate your prayers, too," Sol said with a sigh, "for when I go to see Nina. Don't think I'll be comin' into town for coffee this mornin'. Probably see you tomorrow, though."

Afterward, Sol poured himself some coffee. He carried his cup outside to sit on the back steps, allowing the warmth of the late afternoon sun to seep through to his hide. In times like these he missed old Jake the most. "Used to come lay his head on my knee when he was a pup, rollin' those milky eyes up at me. . . ." Sol had to chuckle as he recalled Jake's antics. "Was good, Lord, havin' that dog around. Can't help missin' him."

He looked up at the tree limbs swollen with buds, then down at the greening of the grass. "Spring. The time, my Friend, when you make all things new again. You can to do that for Frank, too, Lord. He's the most miserable human I've ever known. But you could change all that. You could change *him*. You're the only one who can do it, if he'll just let you. Help Frank, Lord. Draw him to you. And be with Nina and Vic."

Sol sat there leaning against the aluminum storm door Vic and Frank had put up against his will. He thought back over the past months. A lot had happened. His own life, the one he thought he'd buried with Ruth, was opening up again, budding with vigor like the branches of the trees overhead. "It's your doin', my Friend. I've got a church family now. Gettin' along better with Vic than I ever expected. There's Ted, Teddy, and the horses. Perry and Vera, too." Sol had to smile. "If you can change me, bring life back to this old coot, you can change Frank."

Ted was alone when he came that evening to check on the horses. Sol was at the barn brushing Mike when Ted walked in. Not seeing the boy, Sol inquired, "Where's Teddy?"

"He has the flu. He and his mother are both sick."

"A lot of that goin' around, I hear."

They checked on Bell again. "She's getting closer to layin' that foal down," Sol remarked. "I hope it doesn't come while Teddy's sick. I know he'd like to be here."

Ted nodded. "I don't think this old girl's going to wait for anybody."

Vic phoned later that night to make sure everything was all right before leaving early the next morning with Frank. Then, just as Sol was thinking about going to bed, he heard a car out by the barn. He grabbed a flashlight and hurried outside. But it was only Ted, who had come to look in on Bell again.

"I'll set my alarm and check on her during the night," Sol offered. "You've got to get up for work in the mornin'. I can sleep in if need be."

"I don't want you to have to—"

"Now!" Sol stopped him. "That mare and foal are part mine, remember?"

Instead of going to bed, Sol stretched out on the living room couch fully dressed. He awoke before the alarm jingled him alert, hurrying out through the nippy night air to the barn. Both horses were quiet in their separate stalls. Bell stood with her head over the low partition, her nose close to Mike's neck. Sol patted them and then went back to the house, this time to bed.

Ted came by early in the morning and suggested that they keep Bell in that day.

Sol inquired about May and Teddy.

"They're still pretty sick. Kathy's staying home from school to look after them. I'm not feeling so great this morning myself."

After returning from his morning coffee break in town with Perry and the others, Sol decided to walk across the field to keep his promise to see Nina. He stopped in at the barn on his way and found Bell quiet, standing half asleep hock-deep in straw.

Nina came to the back door in response to Sol's knock. "Vic told me he'd ask you to come over." She averted her eyes. "I'm ashamed about the other night, asking you over here under false pretenses."

"Think nothin' of it." Sol felt awkward as he comforted her. "Would it be all right if I came in for a few minutes?"

"Oh!" Flustered, Nina stepped back from the doorway. "Of course."

They sat together conversing about nothing in particular. It was a shallow banter people engage in who have nothing of consequence to say, or who do not know one another well enough to talk openly of things uppermost on their minds.

As he was leaving, he reached for Nina's hand, holding it in both of his for a moment. "Vic picked himself a mighty fine wife when he married you, Nina. If I'd made any kind of effort at all to get to know you in the beginning, I would have realized that right off."

She smiled a weak effort.

"I want you to know somethin' else," he added, releasing her hand. "I'm prayin' for Frank. For you and Vic, too."

"Thank you," she acknowledged, her voice tight.

Later that evening, just as Sol was about to check on Bell again, the phone rang.

"Mister Timins?" a hesitant female voice began. "This is—this is Kathy. Kathy Bowen. Dad told me to call. He can't take care of the horses tonight. He's got the flu, same as Mom and my brother. He wanted me to give you the phone number of a veterinarian he's lined up to take care of the mare in case she has trouble when the foal's born."

"Well, Kathy. . . . I thank you for callin'. But I've always had old Doc Bill up on Mill Creek. He's come whenever I needed help with any of my animals."

"Dad tried him, but he's retired. The only other vet is out of town, which only leaves Doctor Miller."

She waited for Sol to find paper and pencil and then gave him the number, ending with a soft, "Bye." The line clicked and she was gone.

As he turned away from the phone, Sol chuckled to himself. "Wonder which arm Ted had to twist to get her to call?"

When time for bed rolled around, Sol again lay down fully clothed on the living-room couch. He set his alarm clock for midnight and placed it on the floor within easy reach. When it jangled him awake later, he got up to trudge to the barn to check on Bell. He reset the clock when he got back in the house.

His midnight check had found Bell restless. At three she was down flat on her side in the straw. He could see where she had been thrashing around. Her dark body glistened with streaks of sweat. She raised her head to look at him as he came into the stall.

"It's all right, girl. Old Sol's here now."

But it was not all right. *She* was not all right! The foal's tiny hooves were visible under her tail, still encased in its birth bag. But they were pointed wrong. "Should be turned the other way," Sol reasoned before hurrying back to the house to call the vet.

"He's out on another call," a woman's sleepy voice responded at the other end of the line. "And then he's got another emergency after that. It could be two hours or more before he gets to your place."

"Foal will most likely be dead by then. The mare, too, maybe. Who else can I call?"

"There's no one real close that I know of who could come tonight. You might try Doctor Burton, but he's over seventy miles on down the valley."

Sol hung up, his hand still on the receiver. He had to have help! And he had to have it fast. Ted and Teddy were sick. Vic was gone. Perry? No, he couldn't call Perry out from town in the middle of the night. Maybe Ted could come over for at least a few minutes. There seemed no other choice.

He dialed Ted's number. The phone was picked up on the third ring by May. "I'm sorry, Sol, but Ted's much too ill. I would come, but I'd be of no help as weak as I still am. I could send Kathy, though. She helped her father deliver a couple foals when we lived in Iowa."

"Do you think she'd come? She doesn't care much for me and seems to have lost interest in horses."

"She'll do it if I tell her to, believe me, Sol! She's been trying to act so cool, as the kids say, since we moved here. But I think it opened her eyes a little when she saw how her friends reacted to the hayride."

"Well, all right then. I'll drive over to pick her up."

Sol stood there for a moment after hearing the line click. There was someone else who might come. He dialed again.

"Nina, sorry to wake you."

"What's wrong?" Her voice came alert when she recognized who it was.

"I need your help. Can you come right over?"

"What's the matter? Are you all right?"

"Yes. But the mare's down. She's havin' trouble birthin' her foal. Ted's got the flu and the vet can't get here for a while. I'm gonna have to pull it out but I'll need help. Kathy Bowen's comin' over. But it would be better if there were three of us. Could you come?"

There was a brief silence. "Well. . . . If you think I'd be of any use."

"Do you know where Ted lives?"

"Yes, Vic's pointed his house out to me."

"All of 'em except Kathy are down with the flu. Her mother's wakin' her now. I said I'd drive over to pick the girl up, but if you'd stop on your way it would save me a trip."

"Okay. I'll hurry."

"Good girl!" He hung up the receiver with a relieved sigh, his eyes pinched closed in a brief but desperate prayer. "Lord! Help me! Help us."

17

Barriers Fall

"Water," Sol spoke aloud as he turned from the telephone. "Let's see. . . . What else?" He glanced at the window, the night-blackened pane mirroring his kitchen. Morning light was still hours away. Pushing aside a heavy depression that threatened to weigh him down, Sol forced his mind back to the task at hand. "We'll need water for cleanup. And. . . ." He willed himself to remain calm. "Rags. Towels, maybe. Let's see, there's some old towels in the bathroom cabinet."

"Lord! I need your help. And right now!" He brought himself up short. "Don't mean to be orderin' you around."

Sol's mind raced. He would have to have a rope to tie around the foal's legs. It had to be long enough for him and the girls to get a good hold on. There was that section of clothesline on the porch. It was strong yet soft.

With a plastic pail of hot water from the kitchen sink, the towels and rope tucked under an arm, Sol hurried back to the barn. He glanced over the top of the partition at the mare as he fumbled with the stall latch. She still lay on her side. The single light bulb overhead was not giving off nearly enough illumination. Putting the pail down, he headed back to the house for an extension cord and another light bulb.

"Lord God, my Friend, please don't let Bell die," he prayed as he followed the bobbing beam of his flashlight, taking the path at a stiff trot. The night chill nipped his ears and nose. "Those horses have been good for me. You've used 'em to pull me back from the edge where I'd slipped. Show me what to do for Bell and her foal, Lord."

By the time the extra light was suspended above the stall, Nina and Kathy had arrived. Sol was kneeling beside the mare when they came in to peer over the partition.

"Well, come on in here," he ordered. "You can't do a thing standin' out there. But come easy. Don't spook her."

"I've never been around an animal giving birth," Nina remarked as she entered the stall, followed by Kathy. "I can't imagine how I'll be of help."

Kathy remained in the shadows. Sol glanced at the girl. "I know you don't like me much, Kathy. Or this horse. But right now we both need you."

"I didn't say I didn't like you or the mare. It's just that I've got better things to do than fool around horses all the time like when I was a kid."

"Got no time for old people either, I expect."

"I. . . ." She stopped, caught in the trap of her own making.

"I'm sorry," Sol noted. "It's your business who you like and who you don't."

"But it's not that I don't like you." Her voice trailed off.

"I haven't been what you'd call agreeable," Sol conceded. "That don't mean we can't change." He glanced at Nina. "All of us. Right now, though, we've got us a mare and foal to save. Maybe," he grinned at the woman and then the girl, "we'll find we're not such bad human beings after all. Do you suppose?"

With a slight smile Kathy moved into the light, kneeling in the straw beside him. "How long has Bell been down like this?"

"I checked on her about three and a half hours ago. She was restless, but on her feet. The foal wasn't showin' at that time. It's been about half an hour since I found her this way."

The girl moved to Bell's head, running her hand along the mare's damp neck. Rolling her eyes, Bell kicked out with her hind legs, barely missing Sol. "She still got some strength left, at least," Kathy noted. "Maybe she'll be strong enough to help if we try pulling the foal." She looked at Sol. "Do you have a rope?"

"It's there in the corner with that pail and old towels." He watched as she picked up the rope. "I figured that's what we'd have to do. Your mother said you'd helped your dad pull a couple foals. I'm mighty glad you're here."

"So am I!" Nina remarked with obvious relief.

Sol took the rope from Kathy. "I've pulled lots of calf younguns, but never a horse baby." He knotted the rope around the foal's protruding legs just above it's still-soft hooves, padding the knot with a towel. "All right, come around behind me, Nina. All three of us are gonna have to get a handhold on this rope. If we pull together we just might get that stubborn babe out. Kathy, grab on behind Nina. We'd best stay clear of Bell's hooves in case she thrashes about."

He planted himself closest to the mare. "On the count of three, we'll pull easy like. Whatever you do, don't jerk. Ready?"

Kathy and Nina both nodded.

"All right. Here we go. One. Two. Three, and pull!" The three leaned back on the rope, but nothing happened. Bell lay still without moving.

"Okay, let up," Sol told them. "Kathy, you know horses. Go on up to Bell's head. Try encouragin' her along."

Kathy did as directed. Kneeling beside the horse's long heavy jawed-head, she stroked the mare's neck, talking soothingly. "Come on now, girl. You've got to help us. We're trying to get your baby out." Kathy glanced at Sol. "Ready?"

Sol turned to Nina. She looked scared to death. "We're ready. Right, Nina?"

She nodded, her face drained of color. "If you say so."

"Okay!" Kathy brought a hand down on Bell's neck with a resounding slap. "Come on, Bell. Push for all you're worth! Come on now!"

Sol and Nina leaned back on the rope again. Bell's rear legs stiffened, her flanks hardening. Kathy jumped up, and ran behind Nina to grab the end of the rope just as Bell went limp again.

"We got it out a-ways," Sol panted, trying to catch his breath. "But it's turned wrong. Maybe I can move it."

"You're liable to get kicked," Nina warned.

"It's got to be done." Leaving the rope attached to the foal's legs, Sol managed to turn its body a little. Bell kicked out again as he stepped back. "Okay, let's get on the rope."

Time had no meaning for the three as they labored together. Nina's uneasiness faded as she, too, called out encouragement to the exhausted mare. Little by little the foal emerged until at last its head was free and its hips in view.

"Okay," Sol told them, "with the next pull, we should have it."

Kathy looked Sol in the eye with a renewed determination. "Mr. Timins, we've just *got* to get this foal out alive!"

"We're tryin', girl. We're a-tryin'!"

Together they pulled again as Bell stiffened, the rope finally going slack as the foal slipped out onto the straw.

"We did it!" Nina cried in amazement. "We actually did it!"

Kathy grabbed up a couple towels, handing one to Sol. Together they began wiping the foal dry, freeing its mouth and nostrils of mucous.

"We've got us a colt," Sol announced. "Now if we can just find life in the poor little critter after all it's been through. . . ."

"Is it a male or female?" Nina questioned.

Kathy glanced at the woman with an amused smile. "A colt *is* a male. If it was a female, he would have said it was a filly."

"Oh. . . ."

Bell lay still, making no attempt to move as Sol rubbed the colt's limp dark body.

"Aren't you supposed to do something to the umbilical cord?" Nina asked.

Kathy shook her head and ran a hand along the colt's thin neck. "It's best to let it break on its own." She glanced at Sol. "We've got us a good one, haven't we, Mr. Timins?"

"We sure have. But, Kathy, if you don't mind, the name is Sol. Mr. Timins makes me sound like an old man."

Kathy grinned.

"It appears dead to me," Nina remarked, slipping wearily onto the straw beside Bell. She gently stroked the mare's shoulder. "What about the mother? Is she going to be all right?"

214

"I sure hope so," Sol told her. "The vet should be here before long. Maybe he can give her a shot to boost her along."

"What about her baby?" Nina inquired.

Just then a tremble ran through the colt's long lean body. An ear flapped forward like a damp noodle.

"It's breathing!" Kathy exclaimed. "Look!"

Sol stood up, mopped at his forehead with the back of a sleeve. "It sure is. Look at that! We've got us a live one, ladies!"

Nina scrambled to her feet and grabbed Kathy. The two hugged each other, then draped themselves over Sol. "Don't go stranglin' me," he warned, with a gruffness he was not feeling. He laughed then for the sheer joy of the moment, taking each of them by an arm. "I thank you. Could never have done it by myself."

"We're quite a team," Nina noted with obvious satisfaction.

Kathy nodded. "I feel like I'm going to cry."

Sol glanced at her. "I'd sure rather you didn't. Never did know how to act around a female floodin' herself in tears. Besides, we didn't get the job done by ourselves, you know. I was prayin' for help earlier. Was prayin' all the time we worked, askin' God for his help. Was the good Lord who gave us strength and know-how."

Sol bent down to the colt again as Bell raised her head. Thrusting her front legs out in front, she slowly heaved herself up off the floor. The mare turned and nosed the colt, licking his head and nickering low, urgent tones of encouragement. After washing his hands in the water pail, now nearly cold, Sol gathered up the rope and towels and carried them outside the stall. The girls followed, watching Bell nuzzle her new offspring as he tried standing on his rubberlike limbs, only to fall back time and again.

"It has white on three of its legs. Looks just like the mother," Nina commented.

"Yah, but the white on his head is a little wider up by the eyes," Kathy noted. She turned to Sol. "What breed was the sire?"

"Percheron, we're told. A tall black stud."

Nina shivered.

"Cold?" Sol asked.

She nodded. "A little."

"Let's leave them alone for awhile and go to the house to warm up—unless," he glanced at Kathy and then Nina, "you two want to go on home."

"No way!" Kathy declared. "I intend on sticking around until the colt's on his feet and we're sure Bell is all right."

"I'd like to stay too, if you don't mind," Nina said.

Sol smiled. "I'd like it if you both stayed. How about some hot cocoa?"

"Why, Father Timins. No coffee?" Nina teased as they walked toward the house in the dim chilled stillness of early dawn.

"It's a special mornin'. Calls for somethin' special."

The three washed up and then sat in Sol's kitchen with their foam-topped cups. Kathy called home to let her parents know about the colt, telling them she'd be home soon.

The eastern horizon was blushed with pink when the vet finally arrived. By then Sol and his assistants were back at the barn. After checking the mare, the vet gave her a shot and pronounced her weak, but fine.

Kathy decided she'd better go home after he left. Nina said she would drop the girl off on her way back to her own house. Sol walked to the car with them.

As Kathy was about to get in, she stopped. "Mr. Timins. I mean, Sol. I guess I really do still care about horses. And. . . . well, about older people, too."

"I'm glad, Kathy. Glad, too, you were here to help."

Sol went back to the barn after they left. He fed Mike and Bell and then turned the big gelding loose. He left the outside door to the pasture open so Mike could come and go as he pleased. Standing with his arms over the top of the stall partition, Sol watched the colt suck, its legs a-spraddle, the stubby tail whipping the air.

"Lord, you came through for us tonight. I'm mighty thankful. I sensed you with us while the girls and I worked." A tear coursed its way down his check. Hastily he brushed it away. "Must be more tired than I realized," he blustered to himself.

The barn door creaked open and Nina walked in again. "I thought I'd come take another look at them." Sol moved over so she could stand beside him. "He's so big! Seems impossible the mare—as big as she is—could have had all of him inside her just a few hours ago."

Sol nodded. "One of God's miracles. One of many."

She glanced at him. "Speaking of God, Vic told me you've started going to church."

"That's right."

"It's none of my business, but I am curious. Why now when you wouldn't go with your family?"

"Stubborn, I suppose. Thought I didn't need it, but found I do. I've been rightly accused of bein' pigheaded from time to time. Is it botherin' Vic? Me goin' now, I mean, when I wouldn't go with his mother or when he was home?"

She nodded. "I think it is. A little. He said they

217

used to try to get you to go with them. It made him feel like you were deserting them, seeing other kids there with both parents."

The joy of the moment faded. Sol sighed as he turned to Nina. "I'm sorry about those days. I truly am. But beatin' myself over the noggin, feelin' bad about what should have been and wasn't, won't change a thing."

Glancing away, Nina bit at her lower lip. "I shouldn't have said anything." She looked at him again and asked, "Could I go with you sometime? To church, I mean."

"Why, sure. Would Vic come with us, do you think?"

"I don't know. He's talked about the change he's seen in you lately. It's made him think. Made both of us think."

They stood there side by side for a time watching the colt nurse. At last Sol broke the silence. "You know, as long as we're clearin' the air, I probably should admit to somethin' else. I resented you at first. When Vic brought you back to Oregon I wasn't prepared for how young you were. Too young, I figured, for my middle-aged son. And you were a city girl. But I can see now how wrong I was."

He smiled. "I've been wrong about a lot of things. You're a woman any man would be proud to call his wife *or* his daughter-in-law."

She draped an arm over his shoulder. "Father Timins, I do believe you're sweetening up." She then grew serious. "I should have tried harder to get to know you."

"Well, we're on the right track now," he said, patting her hand. "There'll always be things we can't scrub out and live over. But now," he gestured toward the mare and foal, "we've finally pulled together." He smiled, "That was sort of a joke. . . ." Sol turning to face her, and added, "The way I figure it, we'd be better off forgettin' the might-have-been's and get on with the here-and-nows."

He stayed at the barn for a while after Nina left. His thoughts went back to the days when Vic and Janet were little. He could almost hear their laughter reverberating through the old barn as though it were day before yesterday. Sol's mind pictured his two children tumbling in the hay, giggling, playing hide-and-seek.

Janet. His very own little girl with sun-bleached hair, probing blue eyes, and spindly long legs. How he'd missed her when she grew up and left home for college, never to return except for short visits now and then. She probably had no idea of the joy she'd brought him. Lately he hadn't allowed himself to think back to those years. Was there too much hurt standing between him and his daughter, after all this time? Too many fences to mend? Now that he and Vic, and even Nina, were drawing closer, Sol wondered if it might be time to reach out to Janet.

Slowly he walked back to the house as a brisk breeze came up, gathering the clouds to herd them off toward the east. Sol glanced up. The coming wind, it appeared, was bringing promise of a brighter day. Maybe even a brighter year.

Sol took in a deep lungful of air, slowly letting it out with a contented sigh, "My Friend. It's been some time since I came right out and thanked you for my family. I thank you now, for my mother. And, yes, even for the father you saw fit to give me. For Ruth, bless her, and Vic and Janet. For Nina and Janet's husband. And for my grandyoungin's."

Yes, he decided as he squared his shoulders against the buffeting wind, settling his green-billed cap down tight over his balding head, even at his age there was plenty to look forward to. Even though he had botched some things pretty bad.

When Sol reached the house he headed straight for the telephone. After a quick glance in the front of the phone book, he dialed an eleven-digit number and waited.

The receiver was picked up on the third ring. "Hello?"

"Janet?" he shouted into the phone.

"Yes."

"Janet, it's Dad."

"Dad? What's wrong? Has something happened out there?"

Sol chuckled. "Oh, I'd say a few things have happened all right. But that's not the reason I'm callin'. Just thought I'd find out how you and the family were gettin' along. And to say—well." He lowered his voice until it was just barely audible. "I. . . . Straightening his shoulders, Sol raised his voice a notch. "I'm callin' to tell you—to tell you I love you, honey. I always have."

There was a long, uncomfortable silence on the line before his daughter inquired, "Are you sure you're all right? You're not ill, are you? Is Vic okay?"

"Couldn't be better. All of us. But I would like to see you and the family. I was thinkin' I'd fly out for a visit. If that would be all right."

Again there was silence. "Well. . . ." she began, stopping before continuing. "Of course. We'd like to see you. But you've never flown. You've always refused. When Mom wanted you to—"

"I know, I know," he interrupted. "But there's been some changes in your old dad. I'll tell you all about it when I see you."

The Author

Shirlee Evans began writing at home for Christian and other magazines when her two sons were in primary school. After they were grown and her first book was released, she took a job with a weekly newspaper close to where she lives between Vancouver and Battle Ground, Washington. While with the newspaper Shirlee received a Washington State Sigma Delta Chi Professional Journalism award for investigative reporting. Six years later she left the paper to pursue her own writing once again while working during the day at Kris' Hallmark Shop at Vancouver Mall.

The idea for this book came while at work as she observed a couple of older parents and their middle-aged children. "I felt so sorry for those parents," Shirlee related. "One elderly mother, who was close to tears, spoke to me as her daughter walked away: 'I'm the one who used to tell her to stay close and not get lost.'"

Since Shirlee's husband was involved with draft horses, she also witnessed the pleasure of a number of retired men who turned to the big horses as a hobby. It was the blending of these two ideas that brought about the story of Sol.

At first her sympathies lay completely with Sol. But as the book progressed, Shirlee's own father passed away. "There I was in the position of the adult child trying to help an older parent," Shirlee noted. "Horrified, I heard myself saying some of the same types of things to my mother that Sol's son said to him. Such as: 'You've just got to eat more!' I could now see both sides of the situation."

Shirlee writes before going to work and then late into the night after she returns home. Besides her writing, family, and work schedule, she participates in church activities at Brush Prairie Conservative Baptist Church, where she is a member.

Shirlee is author of three children's novels on the Oregon coastal Indians in the mid-1800s, published by Herald Press. They are *Tree Tall and the White-skins*, 1985; *Tree Tall and the Horse Race*, 1986; and *Tree Tall to the Rescue*, 1987. Herald Press also published her 1987 book about a pregnant fifteen-year-old. Entitled *A Life in Her Hands*, senior high school students (through The University of Iowa's Books for Young Adults Program) chose it as one of the most outstanding books of the year, and Choice Books named it Book of the Year.

Born in Centralia, Washington, Shirlee and her husband, Bob, have six grandchildren. Bob, a retired truck driver, does the cooking at night, freeing Shirlee to write.

"She helps me with the horses," Bob explains.

Quips Shirlee, "You might say we're a pretty fair team."